PARENTS
WITH
BROKEN
HEARTS

"Bill Coleman not only helps parents understand what breaks their hearts, he also shares wisdom to help in the process of mending them."

— Tim Robbins, Counselor

"Bill Coleman, like his Lord, is close to the brokenhearted. This book is emotionally freeing and spiritually energizing. Readers will find healing and personal meaning as they put into practice the fresh ideas and clear choices that shine from these pages. They will also discover some ways to help others who are hurting."

— Dr. Paul Welter

"Bill Coleman has done it again. Every book he writes reaches out to touch us where we are hurting."

— Charlie W. Shedd, Author of *Letters to Karen* and *Letters to Philip*

Parents
with
Broken
Hearts

William L. Coleman

Fleming H. Revell
A Division of Baker Book House
Grand Rapids, Michigan 49516

Published by Fleming H. Revell
a division of Baker Book House Company
P.O. Box 6287, Grand Rapids, MI 49516-6287

Printed in the United States of America

Library of Congress Cataloging-in-Publication Data

Coleman, William L.
     Parents with broken hearts / William L. Coleman.
          p.   cm.
     ISBN 0-8007-5600-2 (paper)
     1. Parents—Psychology. 2. Parents—Religious life. 3. Parent and teenager.
4. Parent and adult child. 5. Problem youth—Family relationships. 6. Rejection
(Psychology). 7. Loss (Psychology). I. Title.
HQ755.8.C648   1996
306.874—dc20   96-17544

The LORD is close to the brokenhearted
and saves those who are crushed in spirit.
Psalm 34:18

Contents

Acknowledgments

Parents who hurt are usually more than willing to help other parents in pain. The parents I asked to share their experiences all said yes. They know how deep, mysterious, and agonizing loss can be.

I have changed all of the names and rearranged the events to protect everyone involved. The stories and quotes are accurate but slightly repackaged.

Whether a young person separates himself or herself in defiance for a couple of weeks or for a decade, his or her parents are crushed like a reed. They are stunned and may have trouble regaining their strength.

The purpose of this book is to describe what goes on and to offer hope for a good tomorrow. Hope comes in all sizes and doses. It has to be taken regularly.

I do want to note the contribution made by Compassionate Friends. These parents who have lost children in death helped me see the wider picture of loss and recovery.

On the professional level, I am indebted to my good friend Dr. Paul Welter of Kearney, Nebraska. His input gave me a great deal of insight, though he can hardly be responsible for the finished product.

It takes a brokenhearted parent to know a brokenhearted parent. I hope we will be able to reach out and help each other through this book.

One

It Could Never Happen

What parents would ever dream, while looking at their newborn baby, that this bundle of joy could possibly grow up to a life of rebellion, lawlessness, or even separation from them?

Sitting in the hospital nursery, new parents aren't thinking about calls from a school principal, beer cans strewn across the lawn, flashing police lights, or sleepless nights. Their thoughts aren't crowded with unwanted pregnancies, drugs in jean pockets, or surly friends waiting outside to whisk their child away. They can't imagine sitting in courtrooms, counselors' offices, or corridors of institutions, wondering where they went wrong.

Some parents may never face such dark and agonizing scenes, but too many learn exactly what it's like. And their hearts break. They break while the disastrous behavior is going on; and often they remain broken for years, maybe decades. These parents are left hurt and bewildered over what happened and what might have caused their child's behavior.

How are parents supposed to feel? Should they feel guilty, resigned, angry, vengeful, depressed? Should they keep trying to help their child, even when that child is thirty years old? Or should they simply try to forget about what has happened?

How can parents with broken hearts find hope, spirit, and healing? How can they begin to accept what has happened and prepare to enjoy a fulfilling life for the years ahead?

Parents with broken hearts are much like the survivors of auto accidents or other tragedies.

- They wonder why it happened to them.
- They wonder who is to blame.
- They wonder if they can hope again.
- They worry about their other children or their grand-children.
- They lose much of their zest for life.

Parents who fight the normal battles of adolescence fall into one category. They discipline, negotiate, argue, and struggle for change. They share the adrenaline and challenge of trying to steer a moving vessel: their youthful offspring. A great deal is written about how to help these beleaguered parents stay their course and prevail.

Parents with broken hearts fall into another category. For them the day-to-day struggles may be over. Their child has moved out, may be married, might have a child, might be in jail, possibly is an alcoholic, could be using drugs, possibly blames his parents for everything, needs financial support, can't keep a job, and could deny the faith he was taught as a child. Yet little help is available for these parents.

Brokenhearted parents could experience any of this, all of this, or a number of other terrible disappointments. What makes these parents unique is that their child has passed the rapids of adolescence. The young adult carries the twisted results of misspent teen years. How do parents live with those distorted and painful results?

Ron and Linda described their problem this way. Their daughter, Renee, became pregnant when she was a senior in high school. She decided to keep the child and not marry the biological father. Naturally there were many tear-drenched evenings for the immediate family as they discussed what had happened and why.

After consulting friends and one counselor, Renee came to the conclusion that she got pregnant because of her parents. As she explained to them, since her mother and father failed to teach her birth control, and since her father was frequently away at work, the pregnancy was their fault. The counselor encouraged Renee to confront her parents with this charge.

Today Renee is married to another man and has a second child. She gets together occasionally with her parents for social obligations, but it is fair to say that they are not close.

"How do we deal with this?" Ron wondered aloud. "It's hard to get together for Christmas and Thanksgiving when you know she blames us for the mess she is in. She can't get a job because she has no education, and they're always broke. Are we supposed to help them financially because we didn't teach her birth control? Every visit is simply tension city."

Wherever the blame might belong, the question remains: How are the parents to go on with their lives?

Are they destined to flog themselves forever over the accusation? Should they help support the children to make everyone feel better? Would family counseling reduce some of the resentment? Can they block the entire episode out of their minds and act as if nothing happened?

Are they simply shackled by broken hearts for the rest of their lives?

Caught in the Aftermath

"He lives only fifteen minutes from here." Connie pointed east. "He comes over every once in a while."

Her son Daniel is thirty-two years old and has been an alcoholic since he was a teen. He bums around at jobs from time to time, but they are getting harder to find and more difficult for Danny to keep.

"It isn't that I blame myself. I'm well over that," she continued. "My problem is, what do I do now? If I didn't pay his rent, he would have been thrown out long ago. I won't let him move back here, but I can't simply abandon him.

"It's kind of like a toothache, only much worse. The pain is daily, and it never goes away."

Does Connie have a continuing obligation to help her own flesh and blood? Can she donate money to feed the homeless while she neglects her son in his need? Millions of parents are caught in the aftermath of disruptive and even catastrophic child raising. Some parents divorce after their last child leaves home partly because they cannot sort out their feelings. One parent wants to remain involved and continue to help the errant adult child. The other parent argues to let him or her free-fall and pay the consequences. Mixed into these choices is an array of other baggage concerning what happened, who said what, and why other actions weren't taken. Psychologically and spiritually bruised, two exhausted parents haven't enough energy to maintain their marriage.

Spiritual Wounds

Large numbers of parents are affected spiritually. They prayed for their children. They may have had their children baptized or dedicated. Millions attempted some sort of spiritual training either at home or in a house of worship or both.

Afraid to ask aloud, they wonder, "Where was God when it all happened? Why didn't he step in and do something to stop our raging delinquent?" Any attempt to heal broken hearts must deal with the problems of spiritual pain and disappointment.

The Bible gives hope for those of us who have been cut to our souls. God promised to be close and to help the brokenhearted. We will look extensively at this spiritual dimension later.

As we work through the process of healing, let us claim Psalm 34:18 as our preliminary strength.

> The LORD is close to the brokenhearted
>   and saves those who are crushed in spirit.

For those who have tried spiritual or godly avenues and found them unsatisfying, we only ask that you hang on to this simple premise. As the book progresses, we will deal with the tough issues of faith that most of us encounter (see chapter 16).

Asking "Why?"

These things weren't supposed to happen to us. We can understand why alcoholic parents, abusers, adulterers, prisoners, drug users, or absentee parents would have serious problems with their children. But why us?

Many of us were steady, dependable parents who provided for our families. We went camping, we went to ball games, we bought our children good shoes. Though far from perfect, we thought we supplied all of the essential ingredients. We helped with homework, went to teacher conferences, and poured praise on the little tykes.

Most of us educated ourselves through books and church seminars. We disciplined, set limits, grounded our children if necessary. It's hard to believe we failed parenting. Perhaps we don't deserve an A, but surely we don't deserve an F. However, when the final grade came in, there was a glaring F.

"I may not have won the Parenting Award," said Mary, "but surely I should get a certificate of merit. I was there. I worked at it. I gave of myself. But my daughter acted like I was Wanda the Witch. She still resents me.

"I don't feel totally innocent, and yet I can't bring myself to plead guilty. Every other day I waffle between the two; and frankly, it's a miserable place to be."

Some parents with broken hearts find the remainder of life a bitter pill to swallow. They sulk in depression over what they feel is their great failure. Even if they are close to their other children, the perceived "loss" of the one child is over-whelming.

However, we are pleased to discover other parents who are able to get a grip on the rest of their lives. They have found a measured amount of hope and healing. Maybe a crack will always exist in their hearts. But they have found the inner peace and outer activity to make life worthwhile.

Hope and healing are available for every parent who has suffered a broken heart.

Parents' heads swirl with questions as they try to sort out the problems they have encountered. As each chapter unfolds, may readers be able to see light on their particular situation.

Two

Not Alone

Fortunately my entire church board came to my support," explained a pastor whose son was now away in the army.

"My son did it all. He stole. He got thrown out of school. He got into trouble while on a trip with the church youth group. You name it; he did it.

"At first I was afraid the church would turn on me. I was already disappointed with myself. I didn't think they would want to keep a pastor who had a rebellious teenager. But they seemed to love us all the more."

His story isn't rare. Many solid Christian parents see their children choose the wide path toward destruction. This knowledge doesn't change the terrible facts, but it does make us realize how "normal" we are.

Brokenhearted parents are members of a large and diversified fraternity. Its membership includes some of the kindest, most dedicated and diligent parents imaginable. They are stunned and bewildered at the course their children selected.

Two such parents were evangelist Billy Sunday and his wife, "Ma" Sunday, who experienced the loss of their sons, George and Billy Jr.

George lived in California, where he followed his love for wine and women. He was fond of creating notoriety by driving around with females in his Lincoln convertible along Hollywood Boulevard. While in his late thirties, George either fell or was pushed to his death from a seventh-story window.

Billy Jr. likewise dedicated his life to the pursuit of wild living. After attending an all-night party, Billy drove into a telephone pole in Palm Springs, California. He died instantly.

Neither of these stories tells us anything about the home life of Mr. and Mrs. Sunday. Maybe they were the best of parents, and maybe they were the worst. Most likely their parenting skills were somewhere in the middle, like the majority of us.

But what of the biblical admonition that many of us grew up on and fully believed? "Train a child in the way he should go, and when he is old he will not turn from it" (Prov. 22:6).

Too many parents are angry at God because of their concept of the verse. They feel as if God made a promise and then broke the contract. However, the verse is not a cause and effect promise. Rather it is an axiom or wise saying.

This is the way it usually happens, but it is not a guarantee. The only way this could be a guarantee is if God would take away a child's will. All of us have a choice to be the kind of person we want to be no matter what our training.

Take a brief look at family patterns in the Bible and you will quickly see the jagged edges.

King Hezekiah was a godly man, but his son Manasseh was evil. Late in life Manasseh repented and served the Lord. When he died, his son Amon became king at the age of twenty-two. Amon immediately returned to the same kind of evil his father Manasseh once followed. And the Bible says,

"But unlike his father Manasseh, he did not humble himself before the LORD; Amon increased his guilt" (2 Chron. 33:23).

Where is the guarantee in this pattern? Every generation and every individual must decide if they will follow the Lord. And many do not.

While rebellion and degeneracy have always been treated as tragedies, they are neither new nor unusual. Original sin was rebellion against a heavenly Father, and the practice remains until this very hour.

Acknowledging the Problem

How many young people today are rebellious? There is no way to estimate this with pinpoint accuracy, but a few well-known figures will get us somewhere near a ballpark number. Annually this is what happens among teens:

One million run away from home.
Two million are arrested.
One hundred thousand enter mental hospitals.
One million get pregnant.
Half a million give birth.

Even a casual observer would concede that this list is only the tip of the traumatic iceberg. Millions of other teens are in "trouble" and never make the statistical list. Nor do these figures begin to plumb the depths of family despair. Most parent/child conflicts seem to center on nonlegal matters. These conflicts seldom appear on police records:

- Young adults who never call, write to, or visit their parents
- Teens who have told their parents they hate them
- Young adults who have rejected faith
- Young people who have become alcoholics
- Children who married abusive mates
- Young people who have stolen from their parents

- Children who have joined cults
- Adult children who live for drugs
- Sons who don't support their children
- Siblings who dislike each other
- Adult children who have been told that all their problems come from their parents
- Silent children who never express their frustrations

This is only a sample list. Some parents have a combination of these circumstances. Others have situations that are unique or rare. All together, the number of parents and families affected runs extremely high.

As a father recently told me, "That parents have broken hearts may not be normal, but it certainly isn't abnormal."

It isn't popular to admit that we have trouble with our children. Here's how I found out. While speaking at a seminar in Canada, I asked the group what I frequently ask: "How many of you have trouble with your children?" No hand was raised.

I was disappointed but not shocked.

Out of frustration I said, "Well, I guess I'm the only one who has trouble with his teens."

Immediately hands began to pop up all over the room. These parents had trouble but they weren't going to admit it if I wasn't. Parents aren't likely to volunteer this kind of information if someone is simply going to judge or lecture them. They will, however, become involved if they can find others with similar experiences.

Ask yourself this question: How long would it take to name six parents who are brokenhearted because of their children? Look at your neighborhood, your workplace, or your church. Most of us would need only five minutes to think of plenty who are in the same rocky boat.

Looking for Understanding

Hearing an academic articulate the theory and remedy of parental pain may be helpful, but that is seldom enough. Most parents with broken hearts are looking for someone who understands how they feel, for someone who

has spent more than one sleepless night
has watched a dream fall apart
feels betrayed by someone he or she loves
has felt helpless in the face of needless waste
has tried everything
can't shake the feeling of bewilderment
has wrestled with self-blame and self-doubt
has done something stupid in a desperate attempt to make
    things right
has begged God to change things

These and other experiences make us members of the same club. We are the emotionally devastated who have tried to reconstruct our feelings and go on courageously through life.

Such wounded spirits exist all around us. Many are willing to help while at the same time looking diligently for help themselves. Just knowing that others share our pain is a considerable benefit. That in itself will never heal the wound, but it is important to know that others are wounded too. We have not had a unique thing happen to us that no one else has experienced.

Good parents, faithful parents, outstanding human beings have had hot coals poured on their heads. We are all members of the same human race, often members of the body of Christ, and yet we suffer from this same sense of loss and heartache.

David stands out as a prime example of a father whose son rebelled, broke his parents' hearts, and even tried to kill his father.

Absalom, King David's third son, hatched a revolution against his father. He lied and incited the people to rise up to overthrow the king. Collecting a huge following, he soon had himself anointed king. When Absalom's army met in battle with that of King David, the revolution was quashed and Absalom's army was badly defeated.

While Absalom was fleeing on a mule, his flowing hair became entangled in an oak tree, leaving him dangling in space. Joab, David's general, moved quickly to the spot, and upon seeing the king's son, took three javelins and plunged them into the helpless man's heart. Ten of Joab's armorbearers then finished killing Absalom.

When David heard the news of the death of his errant son, he said, "O my son Absalom! My son, my son Absalom! If only I had died instead of you—O Absalom, my son, my son" (2 Sam. 18:33).

David can understand. He was there. David understands every parent who has ever put his face in his hands and wept, "My son, my son" or "My daughter, my daughter."

Many parents have experienced and still grapple with problems surrounding their children; we want to learn from them so that we too can rise up with strength and courage.

Three

Separation and Loss

Most children experience separation anxiety. They are afraid their parents will leave them at the baby-sitter's and never return. Adults basically have the same anxiety. We are afraid the people we love will go away, reject us, and not return. Each loss in life is difficult when it involves someone we care about and someone who cares about us. The loss of a parent, a spouse, a child are all terrible personal blows if we are connected with them in a loving, caring way.

Parents who have lost a child through death, rejection, or imprisonment share a feeling of terrible separation. The details of their situations may differ considerably, but at the bottom of each of the losses is the misery of separation.

A father once told me, "People think I live in agony because my son is a bartender. I am afraid they miss the point. For the past fifteen years I have reached out my arms to my growing child only to have him reject me. He has kept his distance and remained a mysterious character. His job is of minimal consequence to me. It is our separation that hurts me almost on a daily basis."

Losing the Dream

As our child was growing up, how did we picture him or her in the future? Did we imagine a bright-eyed, energetic teenaged son dressed up for some special recognition? Did we picture the evening when our daughter would introduce us to her awkward date?

And how did we picture our family in the future? Did we dream of our family sitting around a Thanksgiving Day table and laughing together late into the evening? Were we looking forward to playing with our grandchildren?

Something happened to shatter our dream of a whole family. Either death or absence or trouble has left gaps in that family picture. Our hearts are broken—for the child, for the siblings, for the extended family, and most of all for ourselves.

"Incomplete" is the word that fits each of these situations: Todd was killed at sixteen; Emily moved away at seventeen; Richie went to prison at eighteen; Marcia ended her own life at nineteen; Karen is twenty and refuses to contact her parents; Lance is living the estranged life of an alcoholic. None of these scenarios is what the parents had in mind. The family picture is incomplete, their child's life seems incomplete, and the parents' lives are incomplete. And they might always be.

We don't know for sure what the young person had or has in mind. Most likely he or she had another scenario in mind too. What we *are* sure of is that the parents with broken hearts were thinking in another direction. That's why their hearts are shattered.

Brokenheartedness is something we cannot understand adequately until we have experienced it. Studies of robins with empty nests or monkeys with no one left to preen will fall short when it comes to discussing personal loss. A parent whose dreams are being wrecked feels as if his stomach has just been kicked in. No one else can fully understand this feeling of loss.

Brokenhearted parents must learn from other brokenhearted parents. Professionals can add to their knowledge and point toward help; therefore, they might be consulted. But when we are talking about separation from a child, only one who has "been there" understands. A parent cannot know what it feels like to throw his sixteen-year-old child out of the house unless he or she has done it. A father cannot understand what it feels like to tell his daughter, "I don't care if you have no place to live" unless he has said it. Only a parent who has been there can appreciate the agony of staying awake all night wondering where his child is. Who can feel the emotion of a parent who packs his child's things in boxes for the last time?

Almost everyone will have to deal with some form of serious separation and loss eventually. Those who are separated from their children endure a peculiar, even unnatural, kind of agony.

Even parents who have experienced loss cannot totally empathize with another parent. While some losses are similar, no two are identical. Each family has too many dynamics going on for any two to be exactly alike.

Here are a few types of losses:

Death of a child. A life is gone from this earth. The child is omitted from all future pictures.

Death by suicide. The child is removed by his own choice. The reasons leading to the decision may be confusing and are certainly painful.

Confinement. The child is in prison or a mental hospital or other facility for an extended period of time. Confusion and guilt might overwhelm family members.

Moving away. Living over a thousand miles away causes a sense of loss, although visiting the child as often as possible partially alleviates the pain.

Tentative rejection. This person will contact his parents if they respond as the child wants. The child might demand money, gifts, acceptance of lifestyle, or use other manipulative approaches.

Living rejection. A child tries to avoid his parents most of the time if not entirely. On the rare occasion when they do get together, the child seems impatient, hostile, secretive, belligerent, or negative.

Several other losses are not included in our framework of discussion. Runaways, kidnappings, and cult recruitment are all losses with different shades of experience and pain. However, while every loss is different, every loss is the same in many ways. If we love someone, if we are connected to someone, we suffer from the loss of that person regardless of what caused the situation. Voluntary loss and involuntary loss are two sides of the same coin, but both are difficult to rationalize.

There is a significant difference between those who have lost a youth to death and those who have lost a child to estrangement. Parents who are separated from children by death are left with the potential to idealize their youth's lost future. They imagine that the deceased would have been an upstanding, thoughtful, and kind person. In all likelihood he or she would have been.

Among parents with estranged children, the feelings are different. They have lost their idealism. Their child's behavior reminds them that "upright, thoughtful, and decent person" does not and may never apply to their child.

Many parents will admit privately that they wish their child lived in some other town. They never know what might happen—an auto accident, imprisonment, a pregnancy, abuse, or whatever could jump out of the box any day.

These parents don't want any more unpleasant surprises. They are tired of trying to juggle their feelings. Worn-out, disillusioned, bewildered, and aching, they hope this problem is going to end.

Some also admit that they might be relieved if their child died. No one can understand that feeling unless he or she has had it. Many brokenhearted parents have had that feeling. They look for closure. If they don't expect the situation to improve, they secretly long for an end to the pain.

Some parents picture a phone call from the police or a hospital. They may envision a few tear-filled minutes to say goodbye to their dying child. Their imagination takes them to a coffin, possibly a graveside, and to some form of finality. These parents know they will have to wrestle with the memories, but feel no longer able to do battle with the present.

Many parents have said something like this to themselves: "I brought her into this world and I will take her out." Don't be shocked that you may have thought this very thing.

The cry is for closure. Parents want to be happy with their children. They are not prepared to be at continuous war with them. Their own child has become like an abscessed tooth. No longer able to bear the pain, they now wish it could be extracted.

A few years ago a minister shot and killed his famous musician son. The son was believed to have led a drug-racked lifestyle entirely opposite to what his father had hoped. When the son came home to celebrate a holiday, his father took a gun and assumed responsibility for his grown child's life.

Apparently unable to accept his son's different value system, the father wrongfully took action for his child's behavior. Fortunately, while many parents think about drastic measures, most are called back to their senses.

Parents need to understand why they are tempted with such thoughts. They don't want to see others hurt, and they are weary of being hurt themselves. The feelings are normal but unacceptable. Death is not an effective form of closure. Our consciences eventually kick in and remind us of that.

The Lost and the Losers

Separation frequently leads to spiritual awareness. Parents feel their faith challenged. Some become stronger through the experience, and some become bitter; others are simply bewildered. All of us need to be reminded that God is very familiar with our circumstances. Throughout the situation the Lord continues to love everyone involved, both the lost and the losers.

Jesus Christ taught us about God's compassion for the lost. In Luke 15 Jesus tells us that God is like a shepherd who leaves ninety-nine sheep while he goes out to look for one who has gone astray.

There can be no doubt that the Lord is looking for our child. Wherever our child is and whatever circumstances our child has chosen, God searches for him and invites him home. Find comfort in the fact that the Lord, the Hound of Heaven, is in loving pursuit of the person we love.

God feels the way we feel. Often God experiences the same sense of separation that parents feel. His heart also breaks for the child who is lost. When the straying child comes home to him, he will rejoice with tears in his eyes.

Jesus Christ also is heartbroken over the brokenhearted. He journeyed to see Mary and Martha because their brother had died. The Bible tells us he comforted them in "the loss of their brother" (John 11:19). It was no token visit to the grave. We are told how Jesus wept over the separation of this brother from his sisters. Even though he knew they would soon be reunited, his heart crushed under the grief.

God doesn't take sides in a family squabble. Nor is he the neutral referee in a battle royal. The Lord weeps for us both. Parent and child are both losers in a separation. God knows that and calls out in compassion to both. Like a long bridge across the gap, our heavenly Father reaches out and touches each of us at the same time.

Four

Why Children Hurt Parents

Kelsi's behavior was causing her mother to become unglued. The high school junior's continued use of pot, her all-night absences, and her refusal to enter into any decent conversation were more than her mother could handle.

More than once Kelsi's father explained the situation to Kelsi. Her mother couldn't sleep, cried daily, and apparently had lost much of her will to go on. In light of her mother's deep love for Kelsi, shouldn't Kelsi back off with her lifestyle so her sick mother could find some peace?

"Tell her to buck up," the normally tight-lipped Kelsi told her father. "She's a fool to worry about me. I can handle myself. Don't try to pin her problems on me."

This girl wasn't stupid. She could see that her mother *and* her father were suffering. In order to maintain her present defiant behavior, Kelsi had to develop a personal logic that was not logical at all. She needed to wrap herself in a series of lies in order to insulate herself from the truth.

Teenagers often ignore the plain fact that they are hurting someone. It isn't that they don't know; rather they choose to ignore it. The reason they do this may not make sense to the adult reader. The logic of youth at this point is extremely immature.

We get angry at a young person's abuse of the people he or she loves. The abuse doesn't make sense. But it doesn't have to make sense. As we search for the reasons, we must be prepared to abandon logic. Otherwise our hunt will be futile.

If a teenager on the rampage accepted the responsibility for his actions, he would stop his actions. The fact that he doesn't proves that he rejects responsibility.

If his life were a dot-to-dot puzzle, the lines would simply fail to connect. It is not that he couldn't connect them. He chooses not to. For example: Son steals the family car in the middle of the night, hot-rods around, smashes the car into a tree and totals it. Father and Mother are angry, hurt, disappointed, and crushed. Son thinks to himself, "What's their problem? They have insurance. Dad is financially loaded. They can get a car. I'm not hurt. What are they angry about? I'm the one who almost got killed." When he draws lines to the dots, not all the lines reach.

If the young person would allow himself to connect all the dots, he would have to change his behavior. Therefore he denies that his behavior has anything to do with the problem. He rejects cause and effect.

A young man came to me because his girlfriend was dumping him. He and another girl had had sex. "My girlfriend says she's hurt," he said defiantly. "Does she have any idea of what my needs are? I was lonely, this girl was available, and I needed someone. Then my girlfriend gets all upset about it."

His dots all connect to himself. He can't draw the line across to reach his girlfriend. In his extreme immaturity, he refuses to take that step.

A child believes she causes everything that happens. She makes people smile, frown, appear, and disappear. Growing older, she learns that life is interactive and people affect each other. The rebellious teen doesn't like that stage of life and decides to drop the concept of responsibility. So she tries to disconnect. She prefers to think that she has no responsibility for anyone else's feelings.

Self-Centered or Self-Reliant?

We sometimes assume that all teens are basically self-centered. This isn't true. Millions of young people manage their personal affairs and care for others at the same time. Some teens seem to drown in their own needs, while others swim very well. Teens may have self-centered needs, especially as they are discovering their new self. But they don't all become blinded by it. Like adults, teens are self-centered in different degrees.

The totally self-centered teen refuses to humble himself to care for others. When he goes that far, he is in no condition to ask what his parents might need. "Need means me. Need doesn't mean parents. It's too much to think through."

These are choices teens make for their own purposes. Each decides which way to go. Teens can't be expected to be fully sensitive to their parents' needs, but many are partially aware. In fact, some teens work hard not to hurt their parents.

"It doesn't bother me," one teenager claimed as he faced his court appearance. "I can handle it. Just leave me alone."

This teen had convinced himself of two things: (1) I don't hurt; and if I do, I can take care of it, and (2) I am invincible and can see anything through.

That's basic adolescence. Anyone who works or lives with teens already knows this is how they feel or pretend to feel. You have to admire their courage and tenacity. The problem is that they transfer this image to their parents. If a teen feels this way about himself, then his parents ought to feel this way about themselves too. A teen believes if she doesn't hurt, they shouldn't hurt. If she is indestructible, they should be indestructible.

And why does the teen believe that? Because it works best for her purpose to believe it. When told that her mother is falling apart, the daughter says, "Well, tell her not to."

It works for her.

It's good to let the young person know you hurt. She needs information. But don't be surprised if she rejects that information and remains insensitive.

These feelings aren't restricted to rabble-rousers. Terri was fourteen when she became a Christian. She didn't think her parents were Christians, so her local church encouraged her to evangelize them.

First, they fortified her with a set of values. According to the church leaders, her parents were lost, didn't know anything, and needed to be rescued by their teen daughter. Terri, already feeling invincible and above pain, was now also convinced she was superior to her parents. The church assured the young lady that she held the keys to heaven and hell in her hands.

Relationship now became all but impossible for Terri and her parents. Their feelings were of zero significance to this teen. She had a higher calling. If they didn't surrender to her teaching, they would remain forever lost.

Any way of thinking that causes young people to erase their parents' feelings sets up an explosive family situation. We should never encourage teenagers to think of their parents' feelings as insignificant. Too often parents are needlessly hurt by teens in careless pursuit of excellent goals. Some forms of self-centeredness come from otherwise good causes.

Nowhere is the evidence more obvious than among divorced families. Young people seldom connect to the pain their divorcing parents might be experiencing. Typically teenagers are swallowed up in the question of what this divorce is going to do to them. "Will we have less money, no car? What about college? I hope it doesn't interfere with the prom and other big events."

The teen figures his parents created the divorce, which is true. If the divorce hurts, they should call it off. It's that simple in his mind. He has no time or emotional energy to try to understand his parents' pain. There is too much pain in his own life for him to let go and be sensitive to his parents' needs.

If a teen has trouble relating to parental pain surrounding divorce, there is little hope that he or she can relate to the pain over his or her rebellion. The defiant youth would have to get it together for himself before he could feel for his parents. By definition that is an oxymoron. It's like saying, "Why doesn't a rebellious, defiant, self-centered teen start caring about his parents' feelings?" The two emotions are at war with each other. If the teen cared about his parents' feelings, he would, of necessity, stop his irresponsible behavior.

Helping Parents Cope

Parents need to get a grip. In most cases they can expect little help from their teen. They may *never* get any help from the child, but in order to cope with hurt feelings, there are several steps that could help.

Tell the teen. Don't assume that the young person knows she has hurt you. Give her information. "It tears me up when you don't come home on time."

Take steps to change the problem. Never imagine that your child will see that you hurt and adjust his behavior. Though this can happen, it very seldom does. Take action and be specific. Take car privileges away. Ground your child. Tell your son or daughter he or she can't go to the party. Don't be content to let the young person hurt you.

Don't pout. Self-pity is not a helpful way to turn a young person around. Bleeding-heart parents accomplish very little in constructive behavior change. Having declared your pain, rise above it and get on with your life. Parents who pout and display self-pity become ugly figures who accomplish nothing.

Set other goals. Go back to the bowling league. Join a Bible study group. Apply for a promotion at work. Rise above the pain and continue with your life.

"I thought about dropping my Sunday school class," explained a mother whose son was in jail for six months. "I figured I had nothing to teach. Besides, what would the parents of my students say? But I'm glad I didn't. I know now that God uses people who are from imperfect families."

Don't expect anything different. Cursing what you can't change will only make the pain worse. Don't let the hurt drive you into bitterness. A young person may take a decade or more to realize how much pain she has caused her parents. Maybe she will never realize. Don't expect it to change until it does. Then you will be pleasantly surprised rather than continuously frustrated.

Two Dimensions to the Hurt

Parents expect to get hurt. That's the price we pay for intimate and caring relationships. Pain is often another aspect of love. But usually we are bewildered by two dimensions of the hurt we receive from our children. First, we don't understand why a young person has to go so far in the hurt he deals out. And second, why does a child have to hurt his parents for so long, often way beyond the adolescent years?

Not every problem child goes to such extremes. He or she may have two to six years of fitful acting out and then calm down into a normal life. Parents with broken hearts usually have a child who has gone to the outer limits. The youth's refusal to rein in his belligerent behavior is what particularly drains the agonizing parent.

That child fails to face up to the depth of the pain inflicted or its duration. Because of those two dimensions the wounds are frequently difficult to heal.

Five

Letting Go

I need three hundred bucks, Dad, and I need it today." A twenty-year-old daughter stood nervously, her voice cracking.

"Count me out this time," her father answered firmly.

"You don't understand! If I don't get three hundred dollars, I'm going to jail."

Her father looked her in the eye and told her sternly, "I will not give it to you."

How could a dad say such a harsh thing to his oldest daughter? When she was nine, they went to circuses, the zoo, and the park together. He bought her costume jewelry and barrettes for her hair.

It's been a long, twisted journey between those heart-covered barrettes and his refusal to cough up money: wrecked cars, stolen money, all-night drinking, running away, continuous lies, trips to court, and other escapades too painful to recount.

Like most stories, this one didn't take one leap straight from piano lessons to incarceration.

Finally this wiser father decided to let his daughter go. Instead of propping her up again and watching her fall a few feet at a time, he removed his hand. He was resolved to let be whatever was going to be.

We parents know we have to let go. Most of us, however, picture ourselves releasing our children under good conditions. We imagine a cheerful occasion: a graduation ceremony, a wedding, a move to a good apartment, a promising job. We envision the rites of passage as uplifting, hopeful, and progressive.

We parents never dreamed we would let the child we love go into the arms of the police, or into a life of drugs, or to run with a seedy crowd. We are shocked, disappointed, and hurt.

The product appears to be incomplete. Like a cabinet with wobbly doors, squeaky hinges, and a rough, uneven finish, it needs more work—a lot more work.

But the time comes when we have no choice. The product is leaving whether we think it's ready or not. The parental craftsman must say to himself, "This child is no longer in my hands." Why the product has not been completed on time is no longer an issue. It is going out the door no matter its condition.

Not only are the parents' hearts broken, but also their pride. Father and Mother know they could have done better. They wanted to do better.

Forced to face reality, they swallow that pride and remove their dedicated hands and tools. They bite their lips, turn their faces to the wall, and bid the child Godspeed.

They feel like the father of the prodigal son. And they are.

The Illusion of Control

Many of us thought we could protect our children, guide our children, and turn them around if they needed it. When our children were five years old, we could pick them up and carry them into the house. If they played in the mud, we could wash them off and close the gate. Parents have great powers of control over small children.

"I thought I had what it took," a father from Dallas wrote. "I love my son, and I was always home on weekends. I was a loving father who was in attendance. You would think that would do it.

"If my son started to drift into trouble, I was there to set him straight. As with an electronic toy, I was there to make sure he didn't crash into anything. But somewhere I lost control."

There will come a time, sooner for some, later for others, when the controls will no longer work.

Recently a nutritionist told of her dream to control the eating habits of her children. They weren't going to become fast-food junkies if she had her way, and she definitely intended to have her way. Carefully she measured food and dictated each ingredient that went into her children's diets.

Finally they arrived at day school, toting perfect lunches complete with carrot sticks, organically raised wheat bread, and pure cranberry juice. Imagine the mother's chagrin when the teacher later told her how much the other students enjoyed her children's lunch selections. Every day at lunch hour, the nutritionist's children traded their finely balanced meal for the cupcakes and pizza slices provided by their friends.

There is no doubt that we exercise some control, and well we should. But none of us should be surprised that our control is quite restricted in both time and scope. With each increasing year our children reach greater independence. We need to acknowledge and accept that independence whether or not we think they are ready for it.

Releasing Things That Separate Us

We have little hope of mending our parent/child relationships unless we are willing to release the things that hold us apart. Parents need to ask if the object or money is important enough to keep us apart for decades, maybe forever.

"It isn't so much the money," insisted a middle-aged mother. "It's the principle. My daughter asked for a loan of a thousand dollars to make a down payment on a car. That was four years ago.

"She takes trips. She buys other things. But never once has she offered to repay the money. I feel like I've been cheated by my own daughter."

This is a common problem in families. The issue that must be faced is this: Should Mother try to teach her daughter a lesson by remaining steadfast and demanding the thousand dollars year after year? Or should Mother send her daughter a note forgiving her of the delinquent amount? By releasing the debt will she have some hope of dealing with more important and deeper conflicts than dollars?

Forgiving the debt can be extended as an act of grace. At this stage in the relationship, an act of grace might be far more valuable than a demand for restitution. But many parents hold on tenaciously. The unkept promise, the missing ring, the unreturned tools, the stolen heirloom, the unrepented lie, the failure to call, the absence at the birthday party, or whatever. Understandably, parents are reluctant to release the egregious act.

We understand parents who refuse to budge. We also see clearly the damage that is created by an intransigent attitude. Healing is far more likely to occur if we release the object. If we fight to regain the object, we may push the shaken relationship farther out into orbit and make it even more difficult to retrieve.

Andy wrecked the right side of the car and promised he would get it fixed. He never did. Maybe it's time to write Andy a note and let the dent go. With or without a note, the mental and spiritual releasing of things, events, and promises is significant. The place to begin is within our own hearts and souls.

Humbling Ourselves

One of the greatest obstacles to letting our grown children go is simple pride. Whether we let them leave or toss them out, we must come to grips with our own failure. Why didn't it work? Where did we go wrong? Shouldn't we give it one more try? How are we going to tell the relatives? How can she survive on her own without us? It doesn't seem right to release this unfinished, barely civil young person to create havoc in the world.

A parent who lets go has to change the question from one of failure to one of acceptance. We are not saying, "Look at the terrible job I have done." Instead we recognize the fact that we were unable to guide our child in a way he or she did not want to go. We tried, but it didn't work.

Humility is the apex of wisdom when it comes to letting go. Pride says we can still change this person. Humility is the beginning of progress and the hope for a better tomorrow. We cannot; therefore, we will not. That's when we let go.

The father of the prodigal son made that exact choice. Why didn't he force his son to remain at the farm? Why didn't he make his son change? He could not; therefore, he did not.

Peter reminds us that God opposes our pride. However, the Lord shows grace to those who are humble (1 Peter 5:5). By acting with humility, we know we have come close to the heart of God.

Where are our children going? None of us can know for sure. They might be heading straight for the crack house, the brothel, or a life of crime. Possibly they are going to find a Christian friend, a loving pastor, or a mirror where they might get a good look at themselves. Letting go means letting go to anywhere.

The good news is that we ask God to travel with our son or daughter. They won't be going alone. This is the true hope of every believing parent.

During that ultimate conversation, we tell God what we are doing. We are handing our adult child over to our heavenly Father. No longer able to hold her or train her or protect her, we are accepting reality. We pray, please go with her where we cannot go. Please watch over the one we can no longer see. Let her know you love her as we love her.

But we can no longer be there.

This is a gift that the believer has. We rise up in pain and put our faith into practice as much as we are able. We've watched our child get on the bus, destination unknown. We've waved good-bye and asked the Great Conductor to keep an eye on him. Now slowly we walk away and hope the next time we hear from him he'll have some good news.

What did we let go of?

We let go of our dream.
We let go of our control.
We let go of our pride.
We let go of our child.
We let go of trying.
We let go of parenting.

What didn't we let go of?

We did not let go of our love.
We did not let go of our faith.
We did not let go of our pain.
We did not entirely let go of our hope.
We did not let go of our pleasant memories.

Only now are we able to step up and take on the challenge of the next stage in life. Something had to be done before any of us could move on. We had to let go. Soon we will begin to feel some relief and renewed energy. Our spirit may not snap back to where it once was, but at least our spirit will live again.

We had to let go.

Six

Sewing the Guilt Quilt

Accoording to Viktor Frankl, each of us eventually faces the tragic triad. We will suffer from.

1. a fractured relationship
2. feelings of guilt
3. the death of a dream (e.g., a complete family)

Whether by the acts of a defiant and rebellious child or because of death or other circumstances, most humans will somehow wrestle with these stages in life. They aren't pleasant. We don't volunteer for them. However, they are normally our load to carry.

One of our best consultants on the subject is Job. He said, "Yet man is born to trouble as surely as sparks fly upward" (5:7).

Job also taught us, "Man born of woman is of a few days and full of trouble" (14:1).

Some of us can actually be thankful that we have seen as little trouble as we have. But be certain, troubled relationships are the common experience.

In a previous chapter we have talked about the fractured relationship and the death of a dream. The "feelings of guilt" part is tricky. If we accept the fact that we have a conscience, then guilt of one kind or another is an inevitable feeling. Guilty people feel guilt. Innocent people feel guilt. It is hard to have a dynamic, meaningful relationship with a human being without some pangs of guilt.

I should have been nicer; I could have been nicer; I would have been nicer, are all liable to run through our minds. There are a few truly narcissistic individuals who have put their consciences to death. Fortunately most of us do not fall into that pit.

Listening to family members who have lost a child or sibling in death, the listener is immediately struck by how much guilt feeling is evident—imaginary guilt and real guilt, guilt from actions taken as well as from actions not taken, parental guilt, sibling guilt, grandparent guilt, friend guilt, and several other varieties of guilt.

Because life is packed with trouble, life is packed with guilt.

However, the fact that we *feel* guilty does not mean we actually *are* guilty. Suffering causes us to become confused. Too soon we begin to think we are guilty simply because we exist.

The Difference between Guilt and Guilty

Sometimes when I take long walks, I occasionally surrender to a bout of energy and run. Gasping for breath, I promise myself never to do that again. A month or so later I forget myself and jog another short distance, much to my regret. Sporadically I run, but by no stretch of the imagination does that make me a runner anymore than leaping makes me a triple jumper.

In the same sense, one error does not make us guilty. If someone foolishly spends twenty dollars, that simple action does not cause the family to file bankruptcy. The person bears guilt, but he is not guilty for what ultimately happened.

This distinction is extremely important for parents with broken hearts. Because we were engaged in an interpersonal relationship with our child, we also certainly have guilt. We must have done something wrong sometime. But those errors do not make us guilty of creating a wild child.

Not understanding that distinction drives many parents to neurotic distraction. We add up each mistake and treat it as if it were the determining factor. Each error, accidental or deliberate, we then assume made this sad result.

It is true that some parents are major contributors to their child's erratic and delinquent behavior. Child abuse, total neglect, criminal activity, sexual abuse, and other offenses might play considerable roles in misdirecting a child. We would never argue that parents have no effect on their children. But even in some cases of severe parental abuse, the child grows up to be a wonderful person.

Average, normal forms of parental misconduct do not, in fact cannot, create a wild child. We have committed acts resulting in guilt along the way, but we are not guilty of producing this behavior.

(If you, the reader, find this concept too hard to accept, you might want to speak to a minister or other counselor. Brokenhearted parents need to resolve this question as best they are able.)

No one should try to talk us out of feeling guilty when guilt actually belongs to us. That isn't healthy for anyone. But we need to know that if we promised our child that we would refinish her dresser and failed to carry through, that act definitely does not make us guilty of creating an estranged and difficult teenager. The one does not produce the other.

Guilt and Grace

No matter what we think, or whatever our rationalization, we may still feel guilty. Some of us are convinced that we are guilty and do not want to be talked out of it. Unable to rid ourselves of the guilt feeling, the next best thing to do is accept it. Give in. You are guilty. "Phew." Some of us will feel relieved.

It is time to move on to plan B: How does a Christian handle guilt? Turn to God and accept his boundless grace. We messed up intentionally or unintentionally. We have erred, wronged, and sinned. We now have the opportunity to call on the generous grace of God and apply his love to our failings.

In order to do that, we must believe that God has a bottomless vat of grace and that he distributes it liberally. God loves me without regard to my previous or present behavior. Through Christ, God accepts me, forgives me, and welcomes me into his family.

"For it is by grace you have been saved, through faith—and this not from yourselves, it is the gift of God" (Eph. 2:8).

Since we may be unable to differentiate between false guilt and true guilt, there is a time to stop trying. The grace of God is able to cover either or both kinds. Give in. Give up. Ask God to make his grace sufficient for whatever is going on.

Accepting the Agents of Grace

Occasionally a delivery person comes to our house to drop off packages. To this date I have always been receptive and pleasant to the man or the woman who brings them. I like packages. Almost always they contain good things like books or fruit or clothing or something else I enjoy.

Not once in these many years have I tried to run such persons off. I have never threatened their lives, thrown rocks at them, or otherwise attempted to maim them. Why should I? They bring me delightful gifts.

When a kind person attempts to bring us a sample of God's grace, why are we so quick to get the broom and chase him or her away? This friend, neighbor, or whoever came to deliver the grace of God is ready to do a work of grace in our lives. We make a mistake by slamming the door in his face.

If we have a spouse who feels guilt, we have the opportunity to be an agent of grace. By doing kind and thoughtful acts, by saying loving and caring things, we deliver grace to our mate. The act or word of thoughtfulness does not have to be related to our parent/child relationship. A guilt-ridden person needs to experience grace so he or she can remember that grace still exists.

By seeing acts of grace delivered by the people we care about, we may well be rescued from an attitude of despair. The Bible puts it this way, "See to it that no one misses the grace of God and that no bitter root grows up to cause trouble and defile many" (Heb. 12:15).

Many parents with broken hearts stand dangerously close to the canyon of bitterness. We remain in danger of falling off the cliff. The acts of grace offered by friends and strangers alike can become the safety fence that keeps us from that gruesome fall.

It is unlikely that we will succeed in talking parents out of feeling guilty. Like muscles, the harder we pull, the tighter the muscles become. By surrounding the person with love, we may help that parent let go of the guilt feeling.

Seven

Envy and Self-Pity

This is a difficult time for us," a mother told me. "Our daughter's friends are graduating from college. We get invitations to their weddings or announcements about their babies. Each time we receive these, our hearts are torn all over again. We aren't even sure where our daughter is or when she might call."

Can any family with an estranged child escape the heartbreak of comparison? Probably not. We are bound to watch others live out the dreams that we once had for our own child. That has to hurt and hurt and hurt.

Someday you will be standing in a store, and without warning your eye will lock on the young man who is sacking your groceries. Uncontrollably your eyes will fill with tears, and you will look away hoping no one noticed.

The sight of that young man has triggered a memory. You remember when your son used to sack groceries. He had a haircut like this youth. Your son was saving money to buy a car. Today he lives in Kentucky waiting for the statute of limitations to run out so he can come back to your state.

Even when your mind is active with healthy thoughts, the ghosts of childhood past will reach out and zap you. You will be feeding geese at the park with your granddaughter when suddenly it will hit you. This is where you fed geese with your own daughter. Then you choke up.

There are some battles parents with broken hearts might always have to wage. They will struggle with memories, fight to stave off envy, and do hand-to-hand combat with self-pity. Each campaign is unique and may call for a peculiar strategy. Whether we like it or not, each battle must be fought if we are to maintain our equilibrium. To stop is to surrender, and none of us can afford to stop resisting.

The Envy Attack

Under the best of conditions we want what others have. In times of prolonged stress, we envy others all the more.

Sometimes envy takes an even worse turn. Too often we are relieved to hear bad news about someone else's child. When we learn that the mayor's son got into trouble or the neighbor's daughter was suspended from school, our hearts might leap a bit. Not that we wish them ill. Rather we are reassured that our family isn't so terribly odd if other "good" homes have problems too.

Comparing ourselves with others is a slippery business. On the one hand we feel sickened to hear bad reports about others, and yet that same news assures us that we really are part of the human race.

We parents need to keep envy in check, or we can easily slide into destructive behavior. When it comes to envy, the Bible gives us straight talk and instant wisdom.

1 Peter 2:1—Put away all envy; it simply is a terrible way to operate.

1 Corinthians 13:4—Love of others does not permit envy. We start to look at others perversely when we want what they have.

James 3:14—Envy is not a spiritual resource, it is a base desire.

1 John 3:12—Envy distracts us from dealing with our own situation. Cain, instead of facing his own problems, killed his brother Abel because he envied what Abel had.

Few feelings will do more to sap our energy and sour the way we look at others than this demon envy. As Francis Bacon said, "Envy takes no holidays." It will haunt us every day if we give it free rein.

Eventually we will learn to rejoice in the good we hear about others and not in the evil. If we had the power to change people, we would set every family free from the struggle over their estranged child.

Parents who feel hurt about their grown children are tempted to envy parents who have lost a child in death. They imagine that when a child dies in an automobile accident, at least there is a sense of closure. With the rebellious, troublesome, adult child parents are seldom able to rest. Tomorrow they might get a call that their son is going to prison, that their daughter is pregnant and doesn't know who the father is, or that their son has crashed his car and killed someone. There is anxiety and fear of what tomorrow might bring.

They may not wish their child dead, but many admit that it would bring a sense of relief. That feeling might seem strange to those who haven't experienced it; but remember that many parents with broken hearts have carried an unbearable load for fifteen, twenty, thirty, or more years.

The temptation is to actually envy those who have lost children in death.

When I mentioned this phenomenon to parents who had lost their children to death, they said they understood. They realized that people believe the death of a child is the end of something. But for them death is not a sense of closure. They continue to live with the death of their child. Parents continue to weep, to remember, and to work out their feelings. Their child is gone, but the loss remains and so does the pain.

While death may change the problems, it does not remove them. Death brings a different set.

This is part of the problem of suffering and pain. Our ordeal becomes so severe that we imagine that we would like to trade our pile of pain for someone else's. As appealing as that sounds, we would still receive suffering. And in the long run, all suffering must be dealt with; it cannot be bypassed.

Envy's Brother: Self-Pity

As a parent with a broken heart, don't you sometimes feel terribly sorry for yourself? That is a common emotion among parents who hurt. Envy and self-pity are two sides of the "Why me, Lord?" coin. Seldom do we have one without the other.

On a list of useless feelings, self-pity must be at the top. "Poor me" has no constructive value. It is a thumb-sucking retreat from reality. Though perfectly normal and perfectly understandable, it is without redeeming value.

Jonah collapsed in self-pity after his ordeal at Nineveh. His feelings were hurt so badly that he wanted to die. God briskly confronted the prophet about his attitude.

Self-pity leads to destructive behavior. We have been wronged, and we want it corrected, or we will throw a fit. If we throw a fit, someone might get hurt. That someone will likely be ourselves.

Those who look for ways to use their loss for something good must first rise up from the ash heap. Tomorrow cannot begin until we stop saying "Poor me."

Self-pity is like an anchor. As long as it sits on the bottom of the lake, we will never be able to sail free. We are held rigidly to that one spot—the past. Only when we choose to stop feeling sorry for ourselves will we be able to move on with productive, cheerful, and meaningful lives.

Fortunately, God has sent us people who can help us through our toughest ordeals. Some of us meet regularly with such groups or individuals.

When two people with similar hurts find each other, at first they think they have discovered a gold mine. But if all they do is continuously agree about how tough they have it, they have actually found an empty shaft.

Parents need to ask themselves a couple of serious questions: Are our contacts helping us to move on to a meaningful tomorrow? Or are our contacts helping us to merely rehearse the disappointments of yesterday? The difference is vital.

We don't need people who continue to feed our self-pity. Ultimately it is no comfort for someone to sit around and agree with "Ain't things awful?" Caring people help us to move on.

Eight

The Limits of Pain

Being estranged from your child is a painful experience. Few words can adequately describe the feeling. Parents hurt deep down and the pain affects their attitude, relationships, health, and a great deal more. Some parents feel the pain every day. Others experience it as a low-grade hurt that occasionally flares up with unbearable sharpness. While shopping at the mall a mother sees a young lady who appears to be her daughter's age, and suddenly the parent is overcome with grief. Uncertain what might set off pain, brokenhearted parents remain uneasy and tend to distrust themselves.

If someone merely mentions the word *family,* the brokenhearted parent might wince. The word that they believed would always bring them warmth, security, and happiness has now turned bittersweet.

Parental pain is highly individualized. People with back-aches can point to the area that hurts. Those with headaches can locate what throbs. Parents with broken hearts feel pain in any number of locations and in any variety of ways. Some describe it in terms of headaches, sleepless nights, heart-aches, stomach pain, or in terms of pain in their spirit or soul. For others it hurts to pray, hurts to hope, hurts to look at pictures, hurts to celebrate holidays, or even hurts to hold a grandchild. A few hate to attend weddings, visit college campuses, go to family seminars, or watch family themes on television.

Most important, pain is real, not imagined. Parental pain is serious, and it needs to be handled as any form of gen-uine suffering. Every parent with an estranged child should be free to express and accept the reality of the loss.

Questions Brokenhearted Parents Ask

How Long Will the Pain Last?

The time chart of parental pain is totally unpredictable. The pain will last somewhere between two weeks and a lifetime. Some parents have gone to war with their child for a year or two and emerged from those trials as close friends and relatives. Others go to their grave bitter, dis-appointed, and lonely. There is no normal and abnormal parental pain.

Almost anything is possible. Parents who thought they would never be at emotional hostility with their child have spent decades in exactly that state. Others who feared they would never be close to their child again have lived to fish together on the banks of the Wabash or sit side by side in the same pew.

Parental pain can be readily diagnosed. But it can almost never be accurately prognosticated. That's part of why it is so difficult to deal with.

Pain affects parents differently.

What If the Pain Never Goes Away?

We are reminded of Paul's prayer that the "thorn" be removed from his flesh (2 Cor. 12:7–9). The thorn was not dislodged, and the Lord told Paul how to cope with the affliction. If the parental affliction is not corrected today, tomorrow, or indeed ever, how are we to live with pain?

Once we have resolved that this condition may be true, we are ready to look for the best way to live with our situation. Fortunately there are answers to this question.

People all around us live with pain on a daily basis. Some have trouble tying their shoes or trouble standing up straight. Some feel exhausted most of the time or take pills to make it through the day. Some carry splitting headaches to the office, and smile when they want to cry.

Suffering is the human condition. Most people who suffer rise up to face the day. Many sufferers rise up to conquer the day even when it hurts to do so.

Recently I heard a speaker who suffers from back pain. He hurts every day. After two surgeries, he has found little relief; and the medical profession offers him no ultimate solution There is no reason for this gentleman to believe the pain will ever go away. His condition has continued unabated for thirty years.

The speaker said that chronic pain will change us. Persistent, long-term pain will force a person to become different. Remaining the same is not an option. People who want to go back and become their old selves again are wasting their time in dreamland.

Chronic pain forces people onto a new road. The good news is that the sufferer has the power to choose *which* new road. Some select the low road and follow the route to bitterness and dismay. Others change gears and take the high road to strength and fulfillment. The choice is clearly up to the individual.

Paul's thorn in the flesh presented the apostle with a decision. Would he take the high road or the low? The Lord promised Paul that he would find God's grace sufficient in his chronic disappointment. But Paul would have to make a choice to take the Lord's high road.

What If I Can't Change the Situation?

Some things we have the power to change, and some things we don't. In most cases we are unable to alter our child's attitude. Therefore we have to reach a couple of mature, healthy decisions: First, we cannot change our chronic suffering. But second, we *can* change our reaction to our chronic suffering.

How does the continued pain of an estranged or lost child affect us? Does it:

Make us feel like failures?
Make us feel useless?
Make us lonely?
Make us feel confused?
Make us feel like quitting?
Make us want to leave our family?
Make us blame each other?
Make our faith weak?
Make us listless?
Make us lose sleep?
Make us angry and bitter?
Make us afraid to trust?
Make us cheerless?
Make us feel ashamed?
Make us brokenhearted?
Make us morbidly introspective?
Make us jittery and irritable?
Make us depressed?
Make our body hurt?
Make us reclusive?
Make us sad?

If we have these and other reactions to our predicament, there is great news. Everything on that list is curable. Read that sentence again. There is not one thing on the list that cannot be improved. The only part that we may not be able to fix is the loss itself.

Compare that to some of the things we tell ourselves that are *not* true.

"I can never forgive him." That's not true.
"I can never trust again." That's not true.
"I can't get involved." That's not true.
"I can't believe in the Lord." That's not true.
"I can't cheer up." That's not true.

People with chronic suffering can do all of these things. They simply can't get rid of the pain. Consequently, we must choose the high road and rise above the suffering.

What we can't do is rectify the loss. We can, however, get a firm hold on much of the fallout.

The Limits of Suffering

When her daughter left home at seventeen to move in with a boyfriend, Joyce all but quit living. She avoided her friends. Previously she had enjoyed her hobby of painting, but now she could no longer bring herself to pick up a brush. Sapped of energy, Joyce could not bear the thought of taking pleasure in anything.

She did what many of us are prone to do. Joyce allowed the river of suffering to overflow its banks and flood her entire life. Suffering can rage and flow, but suffering has certain limits. Pain is not omnipresent nor is it all-powerful.

Suffering can steal our comfort, but it has no right to wreck our marriages. Pain can restrict the use of our back or our limbs, but it cannot stop us from encouraging others. Suffering is by nature limited in scope unless we allow it to leap its banks and hurt every part of our lives.

Smart parents know that their child's behavior can be potent and destructive. But there are limits to that hurt if parents will keep the other parts of their lives going. If we failed to take an examination to become an insurance agent because our son was getting into trouble, that may or may not be our son's fault. A son's scope of destruction is usually limited. We may have simply *felt* as if we couldn't take the examination while the trouble existed. In fact, we might have been able to take the test and pass it well.

Never give suffering more than its due. This hungry lion will eat up everything it possibly can. But never throw it extra meat. Rebellious children should never be allowed to ruin their parents' romance. They should never be permitted to call a halt to normal family living. Protect your family as much as possible.

"I thought about resigning," Todd said with a sorrowful look. "Here I was, president of the church board, and my youngest son was the terror of the town. It was all I could do to face the board or lead the congregation. I figured they must be thinking, 'Who does this big hypocrite think he's fooling?' I'm glad I didn't quit, but I wrote up my resignation more than once."

Todd's pain was roaring out of its banks. Fortunately he decided to stop it before his suffering was permitted to flood the entire valley. Instead of becoming the father with a broken heart who resigned as chairman, he became the father with a broken heart who continued to lead the church. He accepted the limits of pain and charged ahead courageously.

The son of the governor of a Midwestern state repeatedly gets into trouble. As the child of a famous person, his problems usually get big treatment in the newspapers. According to the papers, this young man was involved in an auto accident in which an older couple was killed. He has been arrested for intoxication, has been charged with using an altered auto license to purchase beer, has had his license suspended, and has been charged with illegal possession.

We don't know if the son is guilty of all of these charges or of none. We do know that the father continued to run for governor and has been reelected. Maybe the governor has recognized the limits of pain. Whatever his son's difficulties, the father has not stopped living.

Pain will rip out whatever it can and destroy it. But smart parents will not let suffering take their spirit.

Nine

The Wheel
of Emotions

How should I feel? That's the cry of the frustrated parent. Their neat little nest is being kicked apart—twigs, feathers, and grass are flying. How is a loving parent supposed to feel when the nest is being torn to pieces?

It's as if the parent is saying, "Help me; I have no experience at this. Tell me how to feel, and I will do my best. Am I supposed to be angry, loving, hopeful, afraid, confident, cheerful, controlled, violent, or what?"

Imagine a sailor whose boat is on fire. Does he fight the fire, collect his valuables, scurry to his passengers' aid, send a message for help, or simply jump overboard? He would do the right thing if he knew exactly what that was.

A parent under pressure doesn't know how to react. Does he punish, forgive, plead, smile, frown, cry, pray, or become cold as ice? Eventually he will probably do all of them. He only wishes he knew which was appropriate at which time.

This book can't tell you how to feel. There are no illegitimate, illegal, or immoral feelings. The best feelings are the honest ones. If you hate your kid, that is honest; you hate your kid. No one should tell you that you don't. If you adore your kid, that is honest too.

Our task will be to help you see where your emotions are. Having seen them, you might then ask where you *want* your emotions to be, by the grace of God. Smart people try to take charge of their feelings. Their goal is not to mask and hide them. Rather, they say something like, "I am filled with self-pity, and I must stop this destructive behavior." That's taking charge. Frequently, we need the Holy Spirit, but emotional control is a distinct possibility.

The Wheel of Emotions

Everyone's story is different. We can't say, "I know exactly how you feel." As much as we would like to say that, it simply isn't true. If we want to know how someone feels, we need first to ask him, and second to listen while he tells us. One of the truly big sins is to shut off a person by pretending to know his emotions.

The wheel of emotions may help the reader find where he or she presently is. From there the parent can ask where he or she might *like* to be and get busy moving to that position.

Some parents with broken hearts may not complete the cycle. That's why I call it a wheel. The wheel might never go around. Briefly let's identify each feeling and see if it matches our experience.

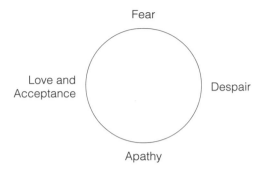

Fear

Our child begins to break away from our family and reject our values. Though this rebellion is usually in the teen years, it often dips to eleven years of age and lower. As the defiance increases in frequency and in severity, parents' fears begin to mount. In the early stages they were bewildered, but the situation worsens and the parents become afraid.

What is happening? How can I stop it? Is our caring family about to fall apart? Are we losing control? Is this simply a phase? Should we get help?

A large part of our fear is the fear of abandonment. Someone we love is pulling away, leaving, and not under good circumstances. That frightens us.

Most parents don't remain at the first level. It's too painful to live for years in continuous fear. The situation either gets better or worse; at least the parent perceives it that way.

Despair

The situation isn't getting better. She stays out later; her attitude is worsening; this is the second time the police have stopped her; she is drinking more frequently. The problem cannot be ignored or tolerated.

We are driven to despair. But despair has benefits. It will force the parents to do something. Let's take the family on vacation; let's get counseling; let's move to another school; let's start checking her homework.

Let's do something to turn this thing around. Like the sailor with a sinking boat, we must do something. Inactivity will surely lead to the loss of the vessel.

Things often must get worse before they can get better. Only when the situation becomes terrible are we likely to take action and try to make something happen.

Apathy

In the movies, people don't reach the stage of apathy. The celluloid parent usually wakes up, finds help, and at last is seen fly-fishing with his grown child somewhere in Montana. That's why we love movies.

My guess is that most people who read this book are hanging somewhere between despair and apathy. Tired of trying, they are about to give up or they already have. Some are looking for permission to be apathetic.

Apathy means "I don't care. I don't particularly love my son, nor do I hate him. I tried feeling both of those ways and neither helped. I don't want to care anymore." That is lifeless, dull, resigned, stoic, unmotivated apathy.

We become apathetic in hopes of protecting ourselves from suffering. It's an understandable, natural defense. We don't want to hurt anymore. Because it hurts to feel, we refuse to feel.

Apathy is not an attempt to correct the rebellious child. It is an act of desperation to preserve *ourselves*.

Love and Acceptance

If our child continues to abuse alcohol, is an irresponsible parent, goes to jail, can we love and accept him? This is a tall wall to climb. The question is: If my son never becomes lovely by my standard, can I love him anyway?

Many of us remain in apathy because it would be too painful to take another alternative. We don't want to go back to the suffering we had when we tried to change our child. But neither do we want to move on to love and accept the estranged child who may never change. Consequently, we remain isolated on the island of apathy.

Someday we might take another look at our child. He may not be any different, but we will see him in that proverbial other light. And we will say to ourselves, "I love him anyway."

Parents can be helped by seeing the grace of God through another person's life. We might feel someone's love toward us when *we* are unlovely. It may take an overwhelming act of love before we are able to lower our guard and love our defiant child. Fortunately this can and does happen in many families.

The temptation is to say that we must love and accept our own children exactly as they are. In truth we don't have to. But if we fail to love and accept, the alternatives are distressing. Our children will find it difficult to call, write, or return to visit us if we cannot love and accept them. Think of how painful it is to contact people who dislike you.

The runaway, move-away, stay-away child is unlikely to hurry home to parents who are filled with fear, despair, or apathy. Parents have to stop trying to change their rebellious child by lecturing him or judging his behavior. Parents who do that are still in despair.

Some parents still live somewhere in the first three stages of the wheel of emotions. They might dwell in the cracks neither quite here nor there. But we have the power to move if we choose to. Otherwise our inability or unwillingness to improve will be injurious to everyone involved.

The important thing is to evaluate where we are and where we would like to be. Then we can ask God specifically what we want to do to change that. The Lord is unlikely to change our feelings or attitudes. God seems to leave our will up to us. But if we decide to make the move, God is more than willing to help.

Parents sometimes dig in their heels and refuse to move. They cannot bring themselves to accept their child's lifestyle.

But as long as they fight over lifestyle, love and acceptance will not happen.

Don't be surprised if the wheel of emotions moves back and forth. Some parents get all the way to love and acceptance, only to slip back to apathy. Their love and acceptance ran thin, his or her behavior worsened, and the wheel went into reverse. Occasionally apathy drops a notch back into despair, and we try again to change our child.

Expect the wheel to remain mobile. Seldom does it lock into position. But if it slides back, the wheel can move forward again. Love and acceptance remains the reasonable emotional goal.

Where Does Anger Fit In?

"I've been angry with my daughter for the past five years," a father told me. "I can barely talk to her in a civil tone. How in the world can I deal with this steamy anger?"

There is good news for this man if he is willing to accept it. Anger is not at the heart of his problem. This is a cosmetic, superficial emotion. The Bible treats anger like a mask that we can rip off anytime we want. That's why we are told not to let the sun go down on our anger. When the sun sets, tear the mask of anger off. Keeping it on is not helpful.

Not that parents don't have cause to be angry. Your son lied, took some cash, and wrecked your car. You don't *have* to feel angry, but it's all right if you do. If a child has been in fifteen years of hell-raising, you have had plenty of opportunity to get angry.

But we have no reason to *stay* angry. Anger should be a brush fire, not a forest fire. Parents are wise if they express their anger verbally when it happens and then put it aside. If we are still angry over the phone bill ten years ago, we have allowed anger to become destructive.

Some of us treat anger as if it were a teddy bear. We hold it, stroke it, and cuddle the furry critter every night. Possibly we have learned to love the anger bear and are afraid to give it up. The choice is a clear one. Do we prize our anger more than we prize a relationship with our child?

We aren't monsters because we become angry. Loss and brokenness are normally accompanied by anger. We have lost something that broke our hearts. Anger can be a healthy expression.

It's much like adrenaline. When fear strikes, our adrenaline pumps rapidly, permitting us to respond to the threat. For a short time we are stronger and faster. But when the danger subsides, we want our adrenaline to retreat to its previous level. So it is with anger.

A large array of emotions is possible for a grieving parent. Most are valuable at the proper time and in the proper amount. Smart parents do not permit their emotions to stampede and run needlessly amok. They grab the reins and gain control. Once in charge, smart parents make their emotions work for them rather than against them.

Protracted anger in parents has little ability to cause our children to create good lifestyles. You may have noticed that few young people will change their behavior as a result of fear.

"For man's anger does not bring about the righteous life that God desires" (James 1:20).

The best emotions are the ones we make work for us. Anger ceases to work for us if it gets out of control or lasts too long.

Ten

Secrets of Imperfect Families

There was a family in Washington, D.C., that I admired very much when I was growing up. The family members functioned well, were generally cheerful, and seemed to care for one another.

One day I took pen in hand and began to make notes about the unit I idolized:

> Dad has a sister who is a forty-year-old alcoholic and who seldom has a job.
> Mother has a parent who has been in and out of several mental institutions.
> Mother has a brother who was dishonorably discharged from the service.

This was the model family that many of my friends wanted to copy or emulate.

Nothing they had experienced eliminates this unit from qualifying as a great example. Like other families, this family is normal and has problems. It has situations to deal with that they handle in reasonable fashion.

Why can't we all have a good family like this one? Most likely we will. We will have a child who will run away, two relatives who will divorce, a brother who will get cancer, an uncle who will get hooked on drugs, and a cousin who will go bankrupt. Generally speaking, this is life.

We need to tell ourselves this so we will know we are normal. Rebellion, disgrace, disappointment, loss, failure, betrayal, anger, and even madness are part and parcel of the human condition. We can expect some or even all of these agonies to afflict our families.

Even the family at church that we admire so much will not be immune from these woes. Some of us will get more affliction and others less. The trowel of grief does not spread evenly, but all of us will receive a heavy share.

It is not our purpose to see how many families we can smear. None of us should seek comfort in the knowledge that the Jones family has one more bank robber than ours.

Seldom is our child's behavior inconsistent with the history of our family tree. Our genealogies are dotted with irregular and outrageous acts. Our problems are often similar to those of our own clan and other families.

"For all of the calamity that my son created, I must admit it was not unlike that of his immediate ancestors. Maybe none of our relatives went to these extremes, but neither is his behavior entirely foreign," a father shared.

"On my side of the family there are many social renegades who were forced to leave town under less than ideal conditions. And on my wife's side it was quite a bit worse. When it comes right down to it, we shouldn't be totally shocked. Disappointed, but not shocked."

The fact that others have gone through similar situations may be of little comfort, but let's take that small comfort, nevertheless. What it proves is that we are not "other." Normal, everyday, sane people with caring relatives crash into brick walls from time to time. We are people wrestling with common problems, experiencing common disasters *and* common successes.

We must have faith in that commonality. To believe otherwise is to imagine ourselves as unearthly monsters of some sort. Our ability to cope will be tied directly to our willingness to say we are normal people who have had a tragedy enter our lives, as normal people do.

We are all torn by similar situations. Not identical but similar. The Bible confirms our commonality.

"No temptation has seized you except what is common to man. And God is faithful; he will not let you be tempted beyond what you can bear" (1 Cor. 10:13).

What tears at my cloth tears at your cloth. What bombards my family bombards your family. The temptations may come in different sizes, colors, textures, and at different prices, but they assault all of us in like fashion.

Keeping Secrets

What are the secrets that hide in the corners of our homes and family trees? Usually we have three kinds of secrets hovering ghostlike from our past:

Secrets that aren't worth mentioning
Secrets we have forgotten
Secrets we guard (like prisoners that we don't want to escape)

Secrets aren't always bad or sinister. Sometimes secrets are pleasant memories that are savored and reserved for one's own pleasure and contentment. Other secrets, however, can be past incidents that we are trying to conceal or paint over, hoping others will not find out.

When I was in high school, I dropped out for an entire year. I came home one day at age fifteen and told my father I would not go back. A year later I managed to find the front door of Eastern High School and continue my struggling academic life.

My children will learn of this for the first time if they read this book. Why haven't I told them before? Until recently I had forgotten about the grief I must have caused my father at that time. When my children were facing difficult times, I never thought to bring that tidbit up to them.

If we look into our past, even our recent past, we are liable to remember a number of secrets. We may have told our family members a few. A couple of arrests or embarrassments we might hold solely for our own amusement.

Many women have had abortions and have not told their families. Some parents were previously married for six months way back when, but never got around to mentioning it. Some mothers were abused as children. A cousin took her own life. A grandfather was severely depressed. One branch of the family had four children with three different fathers.

The value of taking a look at those secrets, maybe even of sharing them, is that they give us perspective. Our family has no tradition of spotlessness, and we may find strength by facing that fact and accepting it.

When we listen to stories in the rural Midwest, one would think all of the family ancestors traveled here as pioneers, each carrying a wagonload of seed and a Bible, and doing honest labor. It makes you wonder who is related to the drunks, criminals, and madmen who came this way at the same time.

Secrets have such a powerful hold on us that their weight is best measured when it is lifted. We don't appreciate how burdensome a sack is until someone lifts it from us. The same is true if we can admit the chinks in our family armor.

When we are able to share some secrets with our family or with others who care, we feel a sense of relief. Maybe we need only admit them to ourselves. Maybe we need to share them with our family so they can benefit from this information. These could be the secrets that our family needs to know to give them a balanced perspective and to help them see more clearly what is going on today.

The Myth of Perfection

The myth is to believe there is a formula available that could lead to a perfect family. Though all of us may accept the fact that there are no perfect families, many still believe the formula exists.

We are deluged with "seven steps to a responsible child," "eight steps to a close family," "six steps to give our child self-esteem," and "five steps to obedient children." The problem with these is that they raise unrealistic expectations. They entice the parent to take the steps in order to produce a certain type of child. Followed diligently, we are told, these steps ultimately will lead to a perfect family.

In reality these are traps that we fall into easily. The formulas say a perfect family is possible. We try the steps and our family is less than perfect. What went wrong? We conclude that the problem must be us. We tried the five steps, and our child didn't become obedient; therefore, we must have done something wrong.

Formulas on how to raise families ensnare us and result in gigantic guilt trips. That's the downside of putting so much emphasis on the family. We idealize it; and when the ideal is not reached, we consider ourselves failures.

The myth of the perfect family exists. The reality of the perfect family exists nowhere. Absolutely nowhere.

The Christian Crunch

For hundreds of years, Christian families have felt the pressure to look good. A solid, intact, even compliant family was a sign of faithfulness and spirituality. Families felt a need to make a happy appearance, even if the domestic unit was flaking away at the edges.

No one felt the pressure more than the pastor and the deacons. Disobedient or rebellious children were a disgrace to anyone holding offices. Today we feel sorry for the poor souls who fought so hard to hide their disruptive children.

Today there is more transparency. Congregations are far more willing to accept a minister with a wild teenager. Pastors are more likely to discuss their problems with individuals, board members, and even entire congregations.

The myth of the perfect family dies hard, but in many places it is acknowledged as just that: a myth. We applaud healthy families, but now we can accept all kinds. If a son rejects his family values or the Christian faith, fellow Christians are less likely to condemn the family. We know it happens. It appears to happen frequently.

There are sad exceptions. A pastor in Wisconsin was recently dismissed from a church mainly because of his son's behavior. The boy's drinking, girl-chasing, fighting, and reckless driving became too much of an embarrassment to the congregation. Some of the teenager's conduct directly involved the young people of the church.

Pastor was a faithful father. Son was a rebellious teen. Unfortunately the entire family had to suffer because of the boy's refusal to comply. Too bad this situation had to cost a good pastor his job.

Another nasty little secret is now out in the church too: Christian families don't always produce Christian children. And sometimes they produce Christian children who live horrendous lives. Seldom do we brag that Christian families are better than non-Christian families. Because so much depends on the individuals, we cannot make that wild claim.

More and more the Christian church is becoming a support group for imperfect families. Christian parents are telling prayer groups that their daughter is hanging around with the wrong crowd. Fathers are telling support groups that their son has a drinking problem or has been arrested.

The veil is lifting, and we see each other as fellow travelers in a dangerous world. This is the beginning of acceptance.

Accepting Our Imperfect Family

A few elementary steps might help any family suffering from severe stress. Try to accept the following facts.

1. My family is not perfect.
2. My ancestry has never been perfect.
3. Imperfect families are normal.
4. I can live with an imperfect family.
5. Many will accept my imperfect family.
6. A few people will not accept my imperfect family.
7. Since I am not perfect and since my spouse is not perfect, I have no reason to expect a perfect family.
8. My imperfect family helps me accept other imperfect families.
9. I need to stop feeling sorry for myself.
10. I have gained strength from my imperfect family.
11. I need to concentrate on the good parts of my family and stop brooding over its weaknesses.
12. Being a Christian does not guarantee me a perfect family.

It's just a list, and it contains no magic powers. But if the points are rehearsed and followed, this list has the potential to change our outlook on our families.

We are in danger of putting family on a pedestal and worshiping this unit. Families are *extremely* important, but they are not everything. When families become everything, we are ill-equipped for any setbacks.

If our families are wounded, dysfunctional, or in disarray, life can go on. In fact, it can go on quite well. If we don't believe that, we lose the will to live when our son joins a cult or our daughter is on drugs. Those are terrible, terrible calamities; but life will go on for those who see life in a broad picture.

God gives us a wide array of reasons to stay involved in life. An imperfect family is never enough reason to pack it in and hate living.

Eleven

Birthdays and Holidays

I think apple pie must be the hardest," a mother told me. "That was always his favorite. Every Christmas I made sure there was an apple pie because it made Derek so happy.

"Now it's too painful. I don't know if he will show up or not. I'd hate to have Derek be here and no pie. And yet if I bake it and he doesn't show up, I will feel sad because the pie just sort of screams out at me."

Birthdays, Christmas, Thanksgiving, Mother's Day, Father's Day, anniversaries, and other special occasions can be miserable experiences to families suffering loss and separation. We look at those times as family gatherings. Now they are reminders that we are *not* a whole family.

It is one thing to have a daughter in Boston who can't be there for the holidays. It is another to have a son across town who refuses to come. And it is quite another to have a deceased daughter whose picture hangs on the wall.

Families tend to fall into two categories. Some try to keep the traditions alive. Others look for new traditions and move ahead. The most satisfying holidays may be the ones where a few traditions are kept, but many new ones are added.

Changing the Routine

The goal is to not forget the person. If he won't be with you, that doesn't mean he never existed. It's unwise to try to erase him from your mind. That's toying with the facts.

A far better solution would be to keep at least one routine that was special to this person. He loved spareribs, so you have spareribs at one meal, though maybe only as a side dish. He enjoyed opening presents before breakfast, so keep that practice and say why. Mention the person, if only once. Many complications arise when a family refuses or neglects to mention an estranged member. There is a reasonable middle where we acknowledge a loved one without dwelling on him. In the long run, the pain will be less if we are not afraid to say his name in a balanced civil tone.

Create new traditions so that the family does not become fixed on sad regrets. If a family tries to freeze itself in the year when she was twelve, they take the chance of being locked in the past.

Acknowledge the person you love but can't have, at least for now. Then move on to be involved with the family members you can presently enjoy.

Extending Invitations

When relationships are seriously strained, misunderstandings become the rule of the day. Is she invited or isn't she? Is the family mad at her? Would they rather she didn't come?

Make it plain. Let her know she is invited. Be warm and sincere. Don't beg. Don't manipulate. Don't bribe. Be direct and friendly.

"We are having Christmas dinner Thursday night at eight. We would love to have you there, and bring your boyfriend with you."

Afterward make double plans. What will you do if they show up? What will you do if they don't? Keep it simple.

Parents may hate the uncertainty of making double plans, but that's the price we pay for a broken heart. We can't have everything neat and cuddly; consequently, we are willing to accept some things in bits and pieces.

Get her a present or put her name in the pool when you draw names if that is feasible. Every family member knows disappointments might lie ahead, but that happens. If he or she doesn't show, move across the situation as smoothly as possible and keep the celebration going.

This is another good argument for giving inexpensive gifts. A five-hundred-dollar gift left unopened is harder to swallow than a five dollar one. The emotional trauma is difficult enough as it is.

Gifts are the least important part of a holiday or birthday anyway. Family, friends, and good food are the memory makers. If we treat gifts as a minor part of the celebration, we remove one issue that might go wrong.

Protecting Ourselves

Parents are hurt often. They have been disappointed, shocked, insulted, perplexed, and crushed. More than once they have been embarrassed. Understandably they hesitate to put their hand out lest the door is slammed on it again.

It isn't unreasonable for parents to learn to protect themselves. Those who thrive on agony need to get their ducks back into order. People who continuously ask for pain and torture should consider looking into counseling.

But we also need to take risks. That's what people in relationships do. Even people in shaky relationships may need to do that. Make the effort even if it hurts. But make it a *measured* effort. Know how far you will go and how soon you will back off.

If all you get is an afternoon a year on a holiday, enjoy that afternoon for exactly what it is. Don't try to make up for all the wounded yesterdays. Don't try to recapture the happier days of early childhood. And don't expect the afternoon to launch you into a miraculous tomorrow.

Enjoy the four hours for precisely what they are—a satisfying afternoon with an old friend.

Twelve

Forgiveness Is Difficult

Does Tyrone have any idea how he has hurt the family?" a mother pondered. "His drinking and lawlessness, his car accidents. I don't think he is even aware of the pain he has caused us. I could forgive him, but I don't know if he has any control over it."

"Sometimes I am tempted to be angry at Lisa," commented a father. "She could have put on her seat belt, and she might still be with us today. Maybe I do hold it against her. I don't know if I have actually forgiven her."

Forgiveness is an important value. Most parents would like to reach deep into the well of their heart and forgive their child for anything and everything he or she has done. It sounds simple enough. It certainly sounds Christian. But brokenhearted parents often have trouble forgiving because the situation is not simple.

Yet if we fail to grapple with the difficulties of forgiveness, our healing and healthy future are seriously in jeopardy. Forgiveness must not be taken lightly.

It is far easier to forgive the Russians, the Internal Revenue Service, or foreign debt than children. We might forgive robbers, gossips, or arsonists. But children are too close and personal to deal with easily. It is hard to accept the fact that our own child, whether flesh and blood or adopted, apparently turned around and intentionally stabbed us, so to speak.

A child is someone we loved and sacrificed for. Most parents can never imagine hurting a child on purpose. But it would appear that our child knowingly and with total disregard hurt himself, hurt others, and hurt his parents. It takes a long time for parents to grasp that, if indeed they ever do.

For years we either accepted or made up excuses for our child's behavior.

It's just a phase.
She didn't mean to do it.
He has no idea how it hurts us.
The problem is her group of friends.
The police are picking on him.
She is a sensitive child.
Teenagers are just like this.
I did some dumb things when I was a kid.

At first we are, understandably, deflecting reality. We don't quite know what's going on, but we think our kid is actually a good kid. If an eleven-year-old continuously hurts family members, parents are reluctant to hold her responsible. Everyone is sure she will grow out of it and become a fine young lady.

We cannot forgive our child until we can say, "This child has done something wrong, and this child is responsible for her behavior." Consequently, some parents of children who are twenty-one, thirty-one, or forty-one years old cannot bring themselves to say, "My child repeatedly, knowingly, and willfully hurts people." That statement is carved over the gateway to forgiveness.

Shirley stood on the front lawn at 11:00 P.M. on graduation night and told her son, "You've got to be back here at 1:00 A.M., and you've got to be sober. If you come in at three or four o'clock drunk, you will hurt your grandparents, your aunt, your dad, and me. Do you understand? One o'clock and sober."

"It's my life," her son replied with anger in his eyes. "It's not my fault if they feel hurt. That's their problem."

With that the nineteen-year-old pivoted and walked away.

His mother still feels confused about the confrontation. Was he acting self-centered and cruel toward his relatives? Did he have an obligation toward their feelings? Was this simply one more in a long list of affronts he had callously committed toward the people who loved him?

Shirley can't bring herself to forgive her son because she can't admit that he has done something wrong. And so it goes with millions of parents who waffle over their defiant child's behavior.

Marcel Proust said early in this century: "We are healed of a suffering only by experiencing it to the full."

We will not heal until we reach forgiveness. We cannot reach forgiveness until we take a long, full drink of our child's behavior and say, "This is foul, rancid, and disgusting." Then we have put one foot on the road to recovery.

Admitting That We Hate

Lewis B. Smedes's book *Forgive and Forget* (Harper and Row, San Francisco, 1984) is a tough and realistic volume. In his chapter on hate the author says, "When we deny our hate we detour around the crisis of forgiveness."

Some of us hate what our child did. We hate what he said. We hate how she treated us. But since he or she is part of our family, someone we love and protect, we cannot admit that we hate that person and his or her actions. Consequently we deny how we feel. If we deny how we feel, forgiveness is impossible.

Middle-aged parents stood by the grave of their younger son. As they cried, each parent felt hate. They hated what he had done. He was drunk when he drove ninety miles an hour and crashed into a tree. He was killed, his girlfriend was killed, and another friend was critically injured.

These parents can bring themselves to admit that they hate what their son did, but they are afraid to ask if they hate their son. Instead, their minds dither around as they try to be sympathetic and understanding. Boys will be boys, they rationalize. He didn't realize how much he had to drink. Maybe his friends egged him to drive faster. He simply had to sow a few wild oats. Lots of boys do this, but they just happen to miss the tree.

Parents are prone to make excuses instead of accepting the facts and admitting their hate. Their clever dodging keeps them from the healing balm of forgiveness.

The message is not that we need to start hating our child. Rather, those of us who *do* hate our child need to accept it, admit it, and move on to forgiveness. The majority of us fit into this group.

We often get angry at people we barely know, like the person who cuts us off on the highway. That anger is usually surface and fleeting. Seldom do we nurse it into deep-seated hate and hold a grudge.

The people we are more likely to hate are those who are near and dear. Hate is frequently reserved for those whom we trust. The people we eat with, sleep with, and to whom we tell intimate stories. When they betray our love and commitment, feelings strike to our heart and soul.

We have been hurt by someone we love. It is quite understandable if we hate the person who inflicted that pain.

Choosing to Forgive

If our son has gotten into trouble with the law, stolen from his sisters, moved to Anchorage, and refuses to accept our calls, we are at a loss as to how to feel. Do we love a son who rejects and abuses us? Do we keep reaching out to someone who never reaches back? Do we speak well of him even when we feel the opposite?

Not knowing how to feel about him, we have finally learned to resent that person. A decade and a half of outrageous behavior brought us to that point. We have steeled ourselves against our own child. Now we are able to continue life protected from any more of his stones and arrows.

Soon after we have fortified our emotions in this mental cocoon of resentment, someone comes along and asks, "Have you ever forgiven your child?"

Horrors! Horrors! Does he have any idea what he is asking? First I loved this child from the depths of my heart. Then I forced myself to admit that my child is a creep who cares for no one but himself. Painfully I settled in and accepted those feelings. Now someone says I should consider forgiving my child.

It's like telling someone that even though emotions have been to sea many times, and even though emotions have sunk every time, you need to pull up your ropes and go out to sea again.

Parents are called to weigh anchor and sail out on the vessel of forgiveness. Afraid of where forgiveness will lead, parents stay on the shore and clutch on to hate or resentment or a false sense of innocence and shiver at the thought of giving them up.

For those who choose to use it, forgiveness is available to help. Those who reject it and opt to hold on to anger are deprived of freedom by their hate and bitterness. Forgiveness is effective only to those who recognize their need for it. No one should try to force us to do something we don't want.

Forgiveness is a radical approach. It goes against our natural gut instincts. Vengeance, self-pity, self-protection, callousness, denial, and hate are the normal reactions. Forgiveness is a spiritual exercise. Even a nonspiritual person has to enter the realm of spirituality in order to forgive. Forgiveness is not the logical bent of the human mind.

If someone hurts us, we naturally feel the need to hurt him back. We want to hurt him in order to protect ourselves and in order to teach him a lesson—unless we decide to rise up to a spiritual level.

Anyone who has been hurt understands the difficulty in forgiving. Forgiveness asks a great deal. Brokenhearted parents understand and are slow to condemn hurting parents who find it hard to forgive their children.

If a parent forgives an estranged child, does that parent have to open up to be hurt again? Not necessarily. A parent can forgive all of his child's past behavior and still refuse to let that child move back into the house. We can forgive a child and not loan him money again.

Forgiveness doesn't mean we surrender our sense of safety. We might forgive an embezzler and yet not make him president of the bank. We might forgive an alcoholic and still refuse to buy him alcohol. Parents can forgive and still be reasonably cautious, careful, and even watchful.

Benefits of Forgiveness

If we can bring ourselves to forgive our child, several benefits will be realized. Each of these could improve our lives today and for the rest of our years.

We won't have to correct yesterday. Sheila lied to the family and embarrassed everyone at the reunion. For years they waited for her to admit her atrocity and apologize. Forgiveness would erase the anxious waiting.

We won't have to unravel everything. A family has never understood how their son could steal five hundred dollars and not return it. Forgiveness could allow the family to stop trying to figure out the incident.

We can enjoy today for all it has to offer. Every day spent with a certain daughter conjures up fifteen years of pain and defiance. Forgiveness lifts the weights and frees us up to make this one day count.

We gain a new sense of freedom. One of the few ways we have to release ourselves and to release our grown child is to forgive him. We want to distance ourselves from our child's actions, but we can never do that until and unless we forgive him. Otherwise we are bound together with barbed wire.

We will find emotional and spiritual healing. Growth will be extremely difficult unless we forgive our son for stealing and wrecking the car five years ago. Our spirit remains tied to the terrible incident that we refuse to let go. We weep over the past because we will not release it.

Spiritual and emotional healing are dependent on our willingness to dismiss the past. We either hold on to the memories or hold on to the person. We cannot hold on to both.

Forgiveness isn't as easy as it sounds. We need to acknowledge that. Pious souls who tell us we must forgive have usually failed to walk in the shoes of a brokenhearted parent. Their glib remarks, easy idealism, prepackaged virtues make it seem as if there is nothing to this forgiveness business.

No, we don't have to forgive. We might decide we cannot stand the pain. But if we are unable to find a way to forgive, we are condemned to carry a great agony the rest of our lives.

The best way to learn about forgiveness is to reach deeply into our own experience. Was there a time when we accepted the forgiveness of our sins in Jesus Christ? Did we welcome the releasing power of a God who cheerfully freed us from our past? Those who have received this gift are able to look inside and wrestle with the serious but difficult questions of forgiveness. God has given us a gift, and now we have the opportunity to give that gift to someone else.

There are parents who cannot forgive because they have never felt forgiven. These parents have a considerable spiritual and emotional handicap. But those who have received God's gift have a point of reference, a deep well from which to draw. "Bear with each other and forgive whatever grievances you may have against one another. Forgive as the Lord forgave you" (Col. 3:13).

As brokenhearted parents, we agree not to judge each other. How parents deal with their defiant child is a fragile subject. Those of us who have made mistakes will be slow to tell others what to do.

However, since Jesus Christ has forgiven us, it is only wise that we consider how to forgive our children.

Thirteen

The Strengths and Weaknesses of Hope

Hope is an easy virtue to tout: "No matter how dark the night, keep your head high and be optimistic." "We don't know what the future holds, but we know who holds the future." A dozen easy and often trite slogans come to mind and roll smoothly from our tongues.

But sometimes these slogans are the wrong thing to say.

Hope has great potential to heal and lift the spirit. However, like medicine, hope can be prescribed at the wrong times and under the wrong conditions. If hope is to have meaning, it must be administered with full caution. When someone doesn't want to be force-fed hope, we should respect his or her wishes.

"My friends used to hit me over the head with hope like it was a hammer," a businessman from Kentucky recalled. "They tried to make me feel guilty because I didn't think things would turn around and blossom like a rose.

"Every year I would get my hopes up four or five times. 'Oh, my son is about to turn around,' I would say. And I would believe it. I did that for fifteen years. That adds up to sixty or seventy times I forced myself to hope.

"Then somebody tells me that I'm a terrible person if I stop hoping. I know more about hope than most people. And I can tell you it hurts to hope."

The message of hope must never be delivered flippantly. People die. They go to prison. They are never found again. They choose not to call their parents. They kill themselves. They die as alcoholics after fifty years of drinking. They abandon their children and are never heard of again.

A blanket challenge to keep our hopes up is sometimes a dagger to the heart. The words, "Don't worry; eventually Megan will come to her senses," can be cruel if spoken at the wrong time.

Distancing Ourselves from Hope

Do you choose to believe that your son will eventually get a handle on his alcoholism and become close to the family again? For those who decide to hope, the gift of optimism can be tremendous strength. But be a realist. Hope might work out, and it might not. Don't think your daughter will turn around merely because you hope it to be so.

The Bible tells a great story about a woman who wanted a child when her husband was old. The prophet Elisha told the woman that the following year she would give birth and hold a son in her arms.

A child was born as the prophet had predicted. As the child grew older, he soon went out into the field where his father was working. One day the child cried out, "My head! My head!" He was carried to his mother, and she held him in her lap. Around noon the child died, and his mother laid him on the bed.

Quickly the mother went to see Elisha who had promised her this son. She said to him, "Did I ask you for a son, my lord? . . . Didn't I tell you, 'Don't raise my hopes'?" (2 Kings 4:28).

The woman felt that her hopes had been played with. At first she couldn't have a child. Then someone said she would. Then she lost her child. Hope had proven to be an unhappy roller-coaster ride.

Hope is a sword we dare not brandish about lightly. If hope is raised and one's soul is cut, it will be difficult to hope again.

At first hope is a fresh new friend. But after years of disappointment, hope becomes a loser standing on the corner in a frayed suit.

"I always thought I would find the answer," reported an aging father. "I had hope coming out of my ears. 'If only I can get him around one more corner,' I always thought. 'If I can get Jason off drugs. If I can get him into college. If I can take him away for the weekend.' There was always one more 'if.' But none of the 'ifs' worked.

"Now I'm out of hope. I need to stop hoping for a while."

After years of chasing hope, some old hounds need rest. The next corner, the next try, the next attempt probably will not work. Sometimes parents need to sit down, catch their breath, and ask if it isn't time to pursue realistic dreams.

Suppose you see a man standing on a pier on a foggy night, and you happen to strike up a conversation with him. Before long you get around to asking him what he is doing there.

"Waiting for the mermaids to come ashore," he replies.

"Mermaids?" You gulp.

"Oh yes, I've been coming here for years. Never met one. But I know mermaids are real. Someday I'll meet one. All I have to do is keep hoping. If a person gives up hope, what does he have left?"

If you are a bright-eyed optimist, a dreamer of sorts, what would you tell this man? Would you encourage him? Would you say that his dreams will come true if he keeps on dreaming? Would that be fair?

Perhaps you should say, "It's good to have dreams. But while you are dreaming, it might be smart to keep working, playing with your children, and repairing the gutters at home. It isn't smart to stand here too long hoping mermaids will come in."

Letting Hope Be a Surprise

After years of trying to change our child's attitude and situation, the time comes to put hope on a different level. Hope is possible. Though hope isn't *always* possible, it is *often* possible. The time may come when we need to stop pushing hope so hard and let it be a surprise.

If your daughter is going to come home and hug you and say she loves you, let it be a surprise.

If your son is going to break his drinking problem, let it be a surprise.

If your child is going to tell you where he lives, let it be a surprise.

The Bible tells us this: "Hope deferred makes the heart sick, but a longing fulfilled is a tree of life" (Prov. 13:12).

If we are sick of hoping because we have always been disappointed, it's time to give it a rest. Let hope sneak up on us at the most unexpected times and really surprise us.

Adjusting Our Hope

The time may have come to take a fresh look at the expectations we once had. Junior isn't going to be president of the student body, and Sally isn't going to sing lead in the school play. We may not have known that earlier, but we know it now. Junior is divorced, can't hold a job, and does little to support his children. Sally seldom calls or writes, and you are suspicious that she and her boyfriend are hooked on drugs. The time has come to adjust our hopes.

We no longer have hope for a responsible child. Our dream is that our child will be less irresponsible. We no longer hope she will stop living with this guy; our dream is that they will give up drugs. If we can't get together this year, maybe we will at least get news that they are well.

Experiences teach us that hope comes in different sizes and in a variety of colors. Hope is available in giant, large, medium, small, and microscopic. The question may not be whether or not we have hope, but rather what kind of hope we have.

We used to dream of camping with our son. Then we dreamed of merely fishing with him. Eventually we wished we could go for a walk with him in the park. Today our hope is that we could sit down and have one civil conversation. Hope and dreams have a way of adjusting, and we have to adjust with them.

A family near Boulder, Colorado, had normal expectations for their son Brad. At first they hoped he would go to college, find a career, and start a family. They looked forward to playing with their grandchildren.

After Brad's numerous bouts with the law, a serious drinking problem, and several wrecked cars, his parents enrolled him in a vocational school. That was good, they thought. Their son could gain a skill in a solid trade.

Soon Brad flunked out of school, was using hard drugs, and had moved in with a woman.

Today those same parents are pleased whenever they see Brad clear-eyed. They are encouraged to hear that he pays his bills. The couple's child belongs to the woman, but Brad is not the father. Brad's parents accept the child as their grandchild and shower him with attention whenever they get together.

Parents may have to seriously adapt their dreams if they are going to continue to hope. Life is a trade-off and some parents need to come to grips with painful compromises.

New Births

There are countless stories of parents who warred with their children for years and eventually found peace. Those are good stories. Each should serve as an encouragement to every parent with a broken heart. Adult children everywhere are turning around and building relationships with their parents.

Peter lives near us. At the age of twenty he capped off a career of hell-raising by serving an eight-month sentence for auto theft. Today Peter has a dependable job, is married, and is the father of a beautiful little girl. The family is sheltered by two proud, doting grandparents. There was a day when no one who knew this young man would have predicted this peaceful scene, least of all the police.

We hear such stories. New births happen to many parents with broken hearts. Like the first birth, it is often painful and prolonged. But when it is completed, both parents accept the gift with joy and pleasure.

Some of the most dramatic turnarounds have come years after the parents had let go. They released their child not knowing where the future might lead. For those who saw the new birth, there is reason anew to praise God.

Ultimately our hope is in God, not in people. God's character never changes. When we go to sleep tonight, we can be certain that when we open our eyes in the morning, the Lord will be by our side.

Fourteen

Marriage Damage

*C*hris graduated from high school in May and left for college in late August. His parents filed for divorce in January. Who would have thought that Cliff and Terri would ever end their twenty six year marriage? What in the world causes people to do things like that?

Actually this scenario is all too common. Cliff and Terri gallantly and vigorously fought the teen wars. Their son all but burned the town down, and they devoted most of their energies to rescuing the lad.

Now Chris more or less has his attitude together, but the war doesn't end. The struggle simply shifts into the lives of his parents. Tired, bruised, bewildered, and hurt, Cliff and Terri don't have enough relationship left to carry on.

Across town live Brenda and Todd; their daughter Marie is serving a year in the penitentiary for theft. They visit Marie once a week. The rest of their spare time is spent raising their two sons at home.

Next month Grandmother will come over to watch the boys while Brenda and Todd go to Minneapolis for the weekend. They plan to see a show, do a little shopping, and spend time enjoying each other's company.

What's the difference between the two couples? Why is one relationship rolling along like marbles while the other has crashed and burned? The answer is not found in their children. Chris and Marie are very similar: Chris is far from being out of the woods, and Marie has a long distance to go if she is going to pull herself together. To discover the difference we have to look closely at the couples, not at their children.

Parents with broken hearts can and do go either way. Marriages under this kind of stress usually become stronger or weaker, but they never remain the same. There are entirely too many explosions, too many arguments, and too many sleepless nights for relationships to stay unaffected.

Understanding the Relationship

There are several factors that help determine which way the relationship will bend. Too many couples fail to discuss those factors. More often they let feelings happen and merely accept whatever fallout those feelings bring. Parents who investigate their emotions and understand them could suffer less marriage damage.

Suffering from Guilt

When one parent or both parents believe they have caused their child's outrageous behavior, enormous suffering will result. The thought that we have personally "ruined" our own offspring makes parents sad and despondent. That attitude is likely to make a parent difficult to live with.

If couples are to survive, they need to resolve any guilt feelings, true or false, to the best of their ability. Counseling or spiritual help may be necessary to gain firm footing.

The Stress of Blame

"You were away too much."
"You didn't talk enough."
"You never wanted to discipline her."
"You always said he'd grow out of it."

Few couples travel through the explosive years without taking a verbal swing or two at each other. Since they believe this situation must be someone's fault, they are bound to occasionally turn on each other. Even if they don't make accusations out loud, they say it to themselves and somehow hold their spouses accountable.

The worst blame is "phantom" blame. A spouse is certain his partner created this turmoil, but isn't exactly sure how. Ghosts are the most difficult monsters to corner and capture.

Couples need to discuss blame and resolve it. Each of us may carry some blame and yet not ultimate blame. Marriages will not prosper if spouses hold grudges against each other.

Different Styles of Parenting

Mary usually wanted stricter rules: earlier curfews, closer checks on homework, fewer privileges, more breath checks, limits on use of the car. Her husband, Bill, was more laid-back. He believed in more freedom at an earlier age. His goal was to have the teenagers make their own decisions and accept the responsibility of those choices.

Frequently parents have diverse views on child raising, and often they are frustrated with each other. Their different styles of parenting come from their experiences, their training, and their personal preferences.

Each parent has plenty of examples of children who grew up with a certain style and who today are fine men and women.

"Kevin never had a curfew in his life and look at him."
"Lisa grew up with lots of supervision and see how she turned out."
"Ted hardly saw his parents and he's a banker."

And so the arguments go. If parents are unable to find some redeeming quality in their partner's parenting style, underground warfare is highly possible. It is best if each parent can find some strength in what the other parent has to offer.

The "Who Looks Good" Award

The counselor looked sternly at the couple and said, "I have to be frank with you both. Mike, if you had spent more quality time with Gary, it probably wouldn't have gone this far. I know it's late to hear that, but I'm afraid you have to face up to the facts."

Karen's heart leapt with each word. She was off the hook, she thought. Even the counselor agreed that Mike messed up. Wow, what a sense of relief.

Karen believes she has won the "Who Looks Good" award. A trained professional pointed a finger at her wimpy husband and blamed it on him.

Many of us are busy looking for that kind of confirmation. We want someone to set us free and indict our partner.

Unfortunately the "Who Looks Good" award is not a marriage builder. Trying to lift our burden at our spouse's expense does damage.

Explaining Your Decisions

There are plenty of mistakes to go around. Under normal conditions couples create enough friction to test the best of marriages. Under extreme pressure they are certain to mess up, say things that shouldn't be said, and make absolutely lousy decisions. All of us have regrets of some kind. If we could do parenting over, we would certainly do it differently.

Parents who are forced to make decisions in the heat of conflict must be willing to discuss the choices they make. They can benefit by talking over those decisions as they are happening. If not, couples need to talk them over soon afterwards. Keep short accounts. Parents who never discuss hard decisions are apt to build up resentments toward each other.

Not that every nit-picking decision should create a crisis. Often you need to make a pronouncement and let it ride. If every decision is second-guessed to death, few actions will be accomplished.

Keeping the Romance Alive

Bob and Laura said they seldom smiled. All of their energies were spent on trying to corral their wild daughter or on worrying about the situation. They had no spirit or drive left to invest in each other.

Their story is typical. Parents are stunned and bewildered over their child's behavior. All of their strength is directed to solving a huge puzzle that only seems to grow more inscrutable.

Smart couples stop at some point, reassess their own relationship, and decide to preserve their love for each other. They also take a close look at their other children and make a vow to protect their good life and sanity. Making choices like that in the heat of battle will be a great help in saving the marriage.

Auto mechanics say we do not change the oil in our cars for the sake of the first fifty thousand miles. We change the oil to protect it for the second fifty thousand. By the same token, parents can ill afford to say, "We will neglect our marriage for the next six years and devote ourselves to Junior. Then when he has left for the army we will renew our romance." By ignoring the needs of the present, we may be wrecking the hope of the next thirty years.

This sounds exhausting, and it is. How can we be all things to all people? Maybe we can't. But neither can we afford to stop our family and pour all of our resources into one individual or into one problem. Relationships often do not survive that kind of overload.

Being Kind and Understanding

Mother is too patient; Father is too harsh. Mother said something terrible; Father promised too much. Mother wants to give him more time; Father wants to throw him out. Mother wants to seek professional help; Father wants him to go to boarding school.

These are typical scenarios. Every parent can remember when the other said or did something with which they totally disagreed. Nevertheless, loving couples try to remain kind and understanding. They still go out to dinner together. They continue to go to church where people love them. They sign up together for tennis lessons. They know their love cannot be shelved for the next five or ten years.

Parents under pressure can read 1 Corinthians 13 and be reminded that

> love is patient;
> love is kind;
> love is not easily angered;
> love keeps no record of wrongs;
> love always protects;
> love always trusts;
> love always hopes;
> love always perseveres.

These are the virtues that jump out to parents with broken hearts. They are the reassurance that love can be sorely tested and prosper in spite of grief.

Righting the Ship

Imagine yourself on a ship riding a tumultuous sea. The continuous rocking soon causes the cargo to shift to one side of the vessel. Quickly the entire crew rushes to grab the loose cargo. As everyone hustles to one side of the ship, it suddenly and dangerously lists to the overloaded side.

The vessel is now in a perilous position. If everything and everyone remains crammed in one corner of the ship, there is a definite possibility that the vessel will capsize. Everyone could be tossed into the ocean if the crew doesn't regain the balance. The crew must quickly move back toward the center and take along whatever it can.

Likewise, if every member of the family rushes over to rescue the erring youth, and the family *remains* there, the damage could be considerable.

Fifteen

Sibling Problems

I suppose I looked the situation over and made my own choice," a young man from Georgia recounted. "My older brother was tearing up the community and making life miserable for my parents. I decided there was more to gain by getting closer to my poor parents.

"Before long I found it easier to tell on my brother. My parents acted like I was special because I kept pretty clean and spied on Evan. Sometimes my brother caught me, but in the long run I got more out of making it look like I was on my parents' side.

"Actually I wasn't all that upset at my brother. He didn't treat me that bad. I just tried to figure what I had to do so I could survive."

Every sibling is affected by a brother's or sister's behavior. That's fairly obvious. What we can't say for certain is exactly how that effect will manifest itself. And we can't know without listening to each particular sibling.

"I hated it," a young woman remembered. "It seemed like each teacher would greet me in class by saying, 'Well, I hope you aren't like your sister.' After a few years like that, I finally gave up and became like my sister."

It probably is true that our siblings have as much or more influence on our lives as our parents. They go a long way toward molding our values and life choices. Not that they predetermine how we act, but they certainly are part of the serious tug-of-war.

Resenting the Offender

Frequently a sibling dislikes his brother's or sister's disruptive behavior because of the pain it brings. The defiant youth usually hurts himself, hurts his parents, and hurts his siblings. Brothers and sisters become distraught and wish they could prevent all three. In fact, they may not be able to stop any of the hurt and are consequently frustrated and angry.

"What I resented most," said Emily, "was how it hurt my parents and what kind of burden it placed on me. I couldn't afford to get in trouble at school or wreck the car because my parents couldn't take any more pain.

"My brother burned the town down, and I had to be a little goody-two-shoes. His actions were so extreme that there wasn't any room left for me to act up.

"I had no desire to compete with my brother even if I could," Emily continued. "The only direction I could go was to try to be as outstandingly good as he was outstandingly awful.

"I went out for sports, was on the honor roll, joined the choir. For me that was the answer to the question, 'You aren't going to be like your brother, are you?' My life would show them that I wasn't like him.

"In some ways it even made me a better person. I think I tried harder because he didn't try at all. Maybe I owe him a little bit for that. But not much."

Generally life would have gone much more smoothly if this brother and sister had been civil. Siblings saw their parents angry or in tears. Holidays were frequently tense and unpredictable. Sometimes rules were stricter because of someone's outrageous behavior. Siblings often felt embarrassed at school, at church, or in the neighborhood. Even finances were more limited because of a wrecked car, extra hospital bills, fines, or other unnecessary setbacks. A cloud frequently hung over the family because brother or sister remained a constant problem.

The last thing in the world teens want is a family member who is weird. They don't want parents who dress funny. They don't want a pink flamingo statue in the front yard. And they certainly don't want a brother or sister who walks on the wild side.

Young people think the pimples on their noses are the size of volcanoes. They believe everyone, absolutely everyone, is staring straight at them. The last thing they want is a sibling who stands out.

It's easy for an adult to say, "Don't worry, everyone knows you aren't like that." That's only a small part of the issue. The teen years are the blend decade. A rebellious sibling makes it almost impossible to hide in a crowd.

Trying to Intercede

Sibling love mixed with idealism will lead many brothers and sisters to try to pull a rebellious youth out of the mud. A few are successful, but the vast majority only get hurt more seriously for their efforts.

"I did try," Ted told us. "I gave my brother lectures. I tried to get him up in the mornings. I threw out the alcohol hidden in his dresser drawers. None of it worked. Finally I just became more angry at him. If I would admit it, I'm pretty bitter today over what he did."

Frequently siblings will attempt to act indifferent. They hate to acknowledge three things: (1) that they care about their sibling, (2) that they feel hurt themselves, and (3) that they hate to see their parents get hurt. If they actually do something to intercede, they are letting one or more of those feelings take charge. Since they are uncomfortable with those feelings, they resent the fact that they have responded to them. This leads to even greater resentment of their brother or sister.

Ultimately, trying to fix the rebellious youth usually results in a strong sense of failure and guilt. The sibling says the upheaval wasn't his fault, but like other family members, he wonders what he should have done to turn it around.

For decades a sibling may wrestle silently with those two uncomfortable positions. On the one hand, he knows he could not have changed the situation. On the other hand, he feels responsible for not having changed it.

At some point siblings need to be told the truth, and the sooner the better. Someone they respect needs to look them in the eye and say it wasn't their fault. They suspect that might be the case, but they still need a firm voice to say it aloud.

Blaming Parents

Children, even teenagers, like to see their parents as big, strong, wise figures. They want to believe parents can solve life's larger problems, especially when those problems center in the home. When this does not happen, blaming the parents is normal.

"My sister quit school when she was sixteen. She was a strong-headed troublemaker. I realize she was going nowhere.

"But deep inside I probably still blame my parents for letting her quit. I know they couldn't keep her in school, and I know they tried. But somehow I see them as weak and failing all of us by not holding her there."

Possibly this is one of the chinks in our parents' armor that none of us wanted to see. And yet all of us see it one way or another. If our parents had been perfect, we think, they could have stopped this. We know our parents aren't perfect, and yet somehow that seems beside the point.

When we hit our late twenties or early thirties, we learn to accept the truth. Our parents may have tried, tried desperately, to change the situation. The fact that it did not improve may have very little to do with our parents' efforts or abilities. The best of intentions are seldom enough to slow down a runaway train. It may simply have to run out of fuel.

Most families will never be able to pinpoint one reason why a teenager went wild. Lots of young people drink alcohol, have trouble learning, have fathers who are away at work, and yet they don't go off the charts with a defiant lifestyle. To say that a family member became rebellious because he started hanging around with a kid named Tyler is too simplistic. Many young people with similar circumstances remain within the boundaries of acceptable behavior.

As long as the precise reason or reasons for the extreme behavior remain a mystery, the family will be uneasy. From time to time we will cast suspicious eyes at each other.

Did his sister spoil him? Did his brother pick on him too much? Was Dad too firm? Was Mom too lenient? Was the school too lax? Were the police too strict? Or was it simply the teen's series of terrible judgment calls?

Occasionally blame raises its ugly head and travels around the family. That uneasy feeling may never go away entirely.

The best hope for siblings is that they accept yesterday as unchangeable. We will not be able to dig up yesterday and fix it. More important is the question of what now. How do we interact and build relationships today?

Moving On

The apostle Paul sets a high standard when he says, "Forgetting what is behind and straining toward what is ahead" (Phil. 3:13).

This doesn't mean families should not talk about prob-lems. Siblings need to air their feelings. Some questions can be dealt with and resolved. Discussions may clear things up without actually finding answers.

At least family members might be able to explain the actions they took or didn't take. Even if the sibling strongly disagrees with that action, at least he or she can hear it out. Even though the total mystery may never be solved, a few clouds might be chased away. Possibly a sibling needs to shout at his father, "Why did you keep giving him the keys?" The mere exercise of expressing what is bottled up in the heart can be of enormous benefit.

Siblings often suffer from a Cain/Abel syndrome. Cain rebelled, acted out, became outrageous. In his defiant atti-tude toward God, he made his innocent brother Abel pay the ultimate price of death. That was unfair. All in the fam-ily suffer when a family member goes too far.

Every suffering sibling should have the opportunity to express his rage at the unfairness of the situation. That won't change history, but it will allow the person to cry out and have a voice.

Sixteen

Where Was God?

A t some point the most important question raised by anyone who suffers loss may be "Where was God?" If we lose our job, watch a child die, get divorced, or have our heart broken in any way, this question bobs to the top: Why did God allow this terrible thing to happen?

Some people all but lose their faith over this mystery. Others are stunned by it. Fortunately, many give it serious thought and come out with an even richer faith than before.

It's possible that the reader doesn't know exactly where he or she will land on this issue. The question deserves careful consideration.

Naturally we look inside to see if we are so rotten that we deserve this sad outcome. Did God pour down his wrath on our family because we didn't go to church enough, didn't give enough, or committed some spiritual transgression?

The answer is a brief one. God almost never acts that way. Basically God is in the grace, love, forgiveness, redemption business. If our heavenly Parent was out to get us, he could bring continuous, unbearable pain. His desire is to be generous rather than mean-spirited.

If revenge were God's practice, he would bring loss to cheats, swindlers, and other malefactors. The fact is that many evil people prosper and many good people hurt.

Do you picture God as a cruel dictator, eager to condemn his children and wrack them with pain? If so, you need to see afresh the loving Father who sent his Son to die for us. The goodness of God is his strong virtue. He loves each person in moments of grief *and* in moments of happiness.

Praying for Change

Brokenhearted parents learn to pray. It's one of those peculiar gains that comes their way. If we haven't prayed for years, the urgent desire returns the first night our teenager fails to come home. And when we pray, we gather up every fiber of hope and faith that we can muster.

Sometimes young people get a grip and turn around, but many times they do not. Some remain renegades for years, and others distance themselves forever.

Eventually we ask ourselves or we ask God why he didn't move in and change the situation. As parents we did what was spiritually right. We prayed. We felt more spiritual. We may have attended church a bit more. We might have given a few extra dollars. Apparently the result of these spiritual exercises was zip. Nothing. Our teen plunged deeper and deeper.

The problem is that we asked God to change another person. God is big on changing people who want to be changed. But the Lord also seems willing to let most people make their own moral and immoral choices. Almost never does God elect to take the power of choice away.

When we pray that the Lord will change someone else, we are almost always praying for the wrong goal. If that worked, we could pray all day for the crooks, murderers, and deviants of this world and see them change their ways on an hourly basis.

We are usually unable to alter our child's behavior by prayer. Prayer has the potential to move mountains, but little prospect for changing other people.

The shame is that parents may see their faith in God wane for a while because of his apparent silence. That's a terrible blow to our spiritual walk, but our faith will most likely return. The reason our faith was bruised is that we believed and hoped we could change others through prayer. That was based on misinformation.

Never again will I pray that God will change someone else.

More realistically we must pray that God will change *us*. By praying that prayer we are laying ourselves open before God and asking for new direction. We are asking for help to become more patient, understanding, loving, firm, steadfast, forgiving, and so forth.

The Lord is more than eager to accommodate this kind of request.

God does answer prayer. Prayer does change things. But most of all, it changes the person who prays. If we understand that, our faith in Christ, our closeness to the Holy Spirit, and our confidence in prayer will remain intact.

Parents with broken hearts will change. They can't go through this much trauma and remain the same. The real question is *how* will they change. The Lord can be a huge help in determining which way we go.

If we turn to the Lord, we can avoid bitterness, despair, and hopelessness. God can help us reach the shores of acceptance, love, and peace. Those are real attitudes worth seeking and achieving. They are part of the fruit of the Spirit and attainable even in the most painful of circumstances.

The Community of Suffering

The Lord has many children who are seriously delinquent and rebellious. He calls them to himself as a hen gathers her chicks, but they will not come. Because of that, God experiences a broken heart.

Parents who suffer a similar loss understand something of what our heavenly Father has endured. To that extent we identify better with that sad corner of God's heart, and he with ours.

We have the potential of being drawn closer to God because we have an added experience of pain. It's called the community of suffering. No one understands a parent who has lost a child in death like a parent who has lost a child in death.

God has many prodigal sons and prodigal daughters. The loss of each, even the temporary loss of each, causes terrible pain. Naturally the Lord understands us, but through this agony we also understand him better.

Encouraging One Another

Parents with broken hearts often see what is most important in life. They know that real values are not material. Materialism fails in times of family loss. At these times many of us are likely to seek spiritual values, which we now perceive as the most worthwhile.

Often parents will become more sensitive to the pain experienced by other families and individuals. We will be more eager to reach out and help steady a faltering friend. We are more likely to hold someone's hand whose child has been arrested, quit school, or run away. It's harder to stand by and say nothing when we have a fair understanding of what they are going through.

Others find spiritual service in teaching a parenting class, leading a youth group, or rounding up a bunch of kids and going places together. These are all spiritual services because they do the work of God as his Spirit moves us to care for others.

One of the worst reactions is for parents to fold up and feel useless because their child is in rebellion. Though we feel like failures, that's no reason to run from God and his service. We may be wounded by this, but it is not sufficient cause for any of us to drop out of a meaningful life.

A Christian speaker and conference leader in the Midwest simply lets the truth hang out. He doesn't tell the gory details, but he lets the conferees know that his family has its share of problems. He even goes so far as to say that there has been trouble with the police. Because he is up front without pouting, many people feel that his ministry is all the more effective. They welcome leadership from someone who has traveled those same rapids.

Today we are more likely to encourage wounded Christians to continue in spiritual service. We are less judgmental and more accepting. God loves the brokenhearted, and many fellow Christians do too.

In the play and movie based on C. S. Lewis's life, the author of *Shadowlands* depicts the famous Englishman as an author ity on pain. He had written and lectured extensively on the subject of how God relates to suffering. However, Lewis's friends were skeptical since he had dealt with little personal pain save the loss of his mother in death. He knew a great deal about the subject, but almost nothing about the experience.

Eventually Lewis married a divorced American mother of two boys. From that moment on, the author was intimately acquainted with love, loss, and pain. Too soon she died of cancer. The school of life taught him a lesson no textbook could offer.

Parents with broken hearts are learning about God in a way they could not have otherwise known. Instead of God and parent rejecting each other, they often embrace one another as fellow travelers on the journey of pain.

Seventeen

What We've Gained

The gain is not worth the pain. Parents aren't glad their child went to prison because the experience taught some valuable lessons. Whatever virtue, whatever strength, whatever insight they may have gained they would gladly give back if they could reshape the past ten or fifteen years.

It's much like struggling to keep your business afloat and finally going bankrupt. When everything is sold and closed, your accountant reminds you that there are some tax benefits coming your way. Naturally you accept the benefits, but you would much rather have had a successful business.

One of the chief characteristics of the Christian life is looking for any good we can find. Many parents with broken hearts can count their blessings despite their grief. Let's take a look at some of those blessings.

We learn humility. During the early months and years we fight for our pride and defend the children we love. No one faults a parent for trying to preserve the family. But eventually we learn how little we can control. Our teenager flunks school, gets arrested, goes to jail, gets pregnant, or whatever. The light of reality shows there is so much that we can't make happen.

Humility begins to set in. We realize how very limited we are. In spite of our education, our experience, our finances, our spirituality, our connections, and our best intentions, there is almost nothing we can do.

It's a devastating feeling. The feeling doesn't come quickly. It's often after the second arrest, the second wrecked car, the second rehab session, the fifteenth check written. We finally understand that we can't change this situation.

Our own sense of inadequacy settles in. We are humbled by our inability to alter another person's life. Our limits scream out to us. We sit on an ash heap and accept ourselves for who we are. "For I eat ashes as my food and mingle my drink with tears" (Ps. 102:9).

We lose our idealism. Parenting is by definition an optimistic act. Whether by birth or by adoption, we welcome children because we believe in hope. We believe in cowboy shirts and patent leather shoes. We believe in piggyback rides and high school graduations.

Now we know that not all dreams come true. We know that life can have a nasty bite to it. But our lost idealism makes us appreciate life's gifts and blessings. They don't come equally, and they don't come automatically.

We become less judgmental. We used to know the answers. We knew what other parents should do. For the life of us, we couldn't understand why they didn't just *do* something. Some of us were glib with solutions like:

"Just take the keys away."
"Not in my house they wouldn't."
"That kid needs to be taught some respect."
"I'd put him in the homework business."
"She wouldn't sneak out of my house twice."

Now we know better. When we hear of a family that's having teen trouble, we feel for them. Sometimes we say something to encourage them, sometimes we pray for them, sometimes we ask if we can help. But seldom do we judge them.

We know there are harsh and mean forces at work. God took the stones out of our hands, and we have no desire to cast anything at anyone else.

We strengthen our marriage. Chris and Brenda from the Midwest said the worst year of their marriage and the best year of their marriage was the same year. Chris said, "I would tell Brenda, 'Look, Rachel won't come home until at least midnight. There isn't anything we can do until then. Why don't we go out to eat and see a movie? Sitting around, worrying about her all evening will only hurt us more.'"

It doesn't work that way for everyone. Many marriages disintegrate under the pressure. Fortunately, some couples realize how much their love for each other means to them.

Children in highly disruptive situations create a volatile atmosphere at home. Sometimes rifts are caused between siblings as well as between siblings and their parents. Often parents do not survive these emotional agonies. Couples who do weather these lengthy storms are thankful for the stronger love they now possess.

Experience can work like strands in a rope. Hardship and disappointment frequently make the cord of love stronger.

We stop blaming each other. "Because we were his parents, we thought the blame had to be found someplace in us," Todd explained. "First, we looked inside ourselves for the answers. Then we decided it was the other parent's fault."

Our society has long taught that children are the product of their parents. We have learned that good traits come directly from them and so do bad traits. If we believe that, we will eventually cast an accusing eye at each other.

"It got so bad," Linda volunteered, "that I was pleased when someone said anything that put my husband down. If someone said, 'You know, Ben doesn't talk much,' in my mind I'd say, 'That's it. If he had talked more, this wouldn't have happened.' Or I'd blame it on his being so frugal. I had to find flaws in poor Ben so I wouldn't take all the blame myself."

Under the most pleasant of conditions it's easy to exaggerate the shortcomings of our spouse. With family stress, we are even more likely to devalue our partner and actually accuse him or her.

In order for couples to survive, they learn to stop blaming. They know their relationship is too important to waste.

We learn how our heavenly Father feels. Parents experience a taste of the excitement God has for his children. But parents with broken hearts have an added insight. They get a glimpse of how a heavenly Father must feel when he is frustrated by rebellious and estranged children.

Estranged children leave a gut feeling that no class, seminar, or study can duplicate. There is no other way to know but to experience it. This estrangement didn't happen to us so we could *have* that feeling. But since we have experienced it, we can now identify with a side of God that otherwise would have been denied us.

Reading the story of the prodigal son cannot compare with living that story. God lives it daily. We have now lived at least part, if not all, of it.

Jesus said, "How often I have longed to gather your children together, as a hen gathers her chicks under her wings, but you were not willing" (Matt. 23:37). We understand that quote now—not in our heads, but in our hearts. Many times we would have gathered our child into our loving arms, but the young person was not willing.

We now have some idea how it makes our heavenly Father feel when we wander away. We also understand more about the joy God feels when we move closer to him.

We are more tolerant. Our bruises have made us more tolerant of the mistakes of other parents. We are not necessarily more tolerant of young people. Many parents with bad experiences think parents should be stricter with all youth.

We know it's hard to be consistent. We know it's tough to make four or five crucial decisions every evening. We know it's difficult to stay ahead of a plotting, deceptive, bright young person who believes all adults are to be fooled.

When a father or mother sits at home, head in hands, crying, we are unlikely to chew that parent out for his or her behavior.

We learn lessons in courage. Soldiers, missionaries, and policemen are supposed to excel in courageous acts. Parents are expected to show courage when doctors in hospital rooms say they have to operate on our children. But little did we know that parents would need courage to answer the phone, courage to confront their own children, courage just to face the next day.

A father in Tulsa said, "I was standing on a golf course around the fifth hole when I happened to look toward the clubhouse and see a police car pull into the lot. Instinctively I thought, 'Oh, no, what now?'

"'Why else would there be a police car except that my son is in trouble again, and they have come for me?' The policeman wasn't looking for me at all. I remained shaken for the rest of the round even after the police car drove away.

"Every day I needed to dig up the courage to go on with a normal life. Some days I didn't want to deal with the uncertainties and the fears, but I had to find a way."

Courage is only a topic of conversation until we are forced to call on its power. Highly rebellious young people make us grapple with virtues we want to ignore.

We wrestle with forgiveness. The brokenhearted are forced to try to make sense out of forgiveness, even though we probably never master it. Whom do we forgive? When do we forgive? How do we forgive someone who has not yet changed his ways? Do we forgive someone who doesn't even want to be forgiven? Does God forgive us based on our ability or willingness to forgive our own children?

Everyone is for forgiveness. The basis of our Christian faith is that we are the forgiven. But when we feel hurt, betrayed, abused, and mistreated, forgiveness is hard to wrestle with—especially when foolish actions are continuing.

Corrie ten Boom taught a valuable lesson about forgiveness. She said she learned to forgive the prison guards while she was still in the concentration camp. She didn't wait until she was free and then forgive them upon reflection. The grace of God allowed her to forgive them in the middle of their acts of cruelty.

Christ forgave his tormentors while he was being crucified. His example calls us to an incredibly high standard. He also helps free us from the burden we carry when we refuse to forgive.

However successful or unsuccessful we may be, we have been given an opportunity to have one of life's richest experiences. We have felt pain while we held forgiveness in our hands and tried to decide what to do with it. Without this agony, we may never have been called on to make that vital decision.

To this extent rebellious, even defiant children have brought true wealth to our souls. Not that we wanted it. Not that we have made the best use of these virtues. But we can be grateful for the side benefits.

Automobile accidents make us more cautious. Lost investments make us wiser. Pulled muscles make us careful. In the same way, belligerent children can make us stronger. Each parent has to decide how much he or she will draw on this newfound character.

"If the truth were known," wrote a man from Omaha, "I owe my son a great deal. For all the pain he brought into our lives, his actions opened the doors so blessings could fly in at the same time.

"I will probably never be able to explain it to him correctly. I probably will never try. But in a backhanded sort of way, he has blessed my life. He made me a better person.

"He changed the way I see others. My values aren't the same. I wish I could have learned the same lessons while he was a good kid, but that route was closed to me. Nevertheless I am, begrudgingly, grateful for the good that his bad behavior brought my way."

Eighteen

If They Had Advice to Give

Advice isn't easy to give or to accept. Many parents in stress struggle to find their own path through the ordeal. Only after the storm has passed do they wish good advice had been available.

But there are exceptions. Some parents are looking for guidance from other parents, and they are willing to try it. For their sake, I have asked brokenhearted parents what advice they might give.

Brokenhearted parents have learned a great deal. Out of their experiences came a dozen suggestions for parents who are in the early stages of the battle. The advice below is in no particular order of importance.

1. Let your child fail early. This is hard advice for parents of a fourteen-year-old rebellious child. Parents try so hard to keep their children from pain.

But that's a serious mistake. If a teenager breaks something, that same teen must take a major role in fixing it.

"I fought hard to make sure he graduated from high school. He drank, didn't go to class, flunked exams, and generally ignored the system. Looking back, I know it was a loss of reality to try and prop him up and keep him from the consequences of his misbehavior," a parent told us.

This is a difficult decision. Some teens snap out of their rebellion. Others merely bounce from problem to problem. At some point a parent has to decide when to remove the safety nets.

2. Use tough love. In danger of becoming a worn-out phrase, tough love is nevertheless true. One father said, "Take the car keys away whether they hate you or not. Many times we should have."

It's hard to be tough with someone you love. Most of us think if we give love, we will receive love in return. When we give love to our child and get contempt in return, the transaction throws us.

Love forces itself to draw a line and makes itself keep that line.

"The first time he stayed out all night," a mother told us, "I disciplined him a little. He thought that was no big deal, so a few weeks later he did it again. Then I said, 'No more nice guy,' and laid down the law. Until then I thought that if I treated him nice, he'd treat me nice."

3. Reduce expectations. Every family expects a neat little unit. None of us planned to be the Ma Barker family with children running around robbing banks. We planned on a bouncy, pleasant, caring flock.

We need to accept the facts. Half of our children may divorce. One of our children may get arrested or pregnant or both. Our children are likely to try drugs. They might marry someone who will avoid your family. A loving twenty-year-old might suddenly change dispositions and blame her parents for ruining her life. A son might move across the country and not contact you for five years.

It happens all the time.

We shouldn't think our family is too good, too loving, too Christian, too educated, too middle-class, or too anything for this to occur. The average, normal family has problems.

The kid we think is an excellent student and responsible person at age eleven could later turn any way he or she chooses to go. Remember, life could take a sudden jolt.

4. *Live one day at a time.* Is the sun shining? Can you do something you would enjoy with your spouse or a child? Do it today. There is no telling what you might have to deal with tonight or tomorrow. Don't live in fear, but be careful to use the goodness you can find in this present hour.

The Book of Proverbs teaches us this: "Do not boast about tomorrow, for you do not know what a day may bring forth" (27:1).

Every distressed parent knows the truth of this passage. Each day can be filled with its own surprises and disappointments. Don't live desperately, grasping at every hour. Instead live gladly, knowing how important the present moment is.

5. *Communicate clearly.* Say what you mean and mean what you say. Many parents are literally afraid to talk.

We don't know what to say.
We are afraid we will say too much.
We are afraid we will say too little.
We are afraid we will cry or shout.

We are held as verbal hostages. Our child's misbehavior so intimidates us that we are afraid anything we say will be held against us.

Parents are often reluctant to say what they really feel because they don't want to have to eat their words. A parent might be angry, confused, disappointed, fed up, frustrated.

She may believe she is being treated like trash. But she doesn't want to say any of that. Too often we swallow our words and fail to share our feelings.

Every child needs to know how his or her parents feel. Children have a right to hear the pleasant feelings. They also have an absolute, rock-bottom need to hear the bad news.

Start off in small chunks, if necessary. Move from words to sentences to paragraphs. Everyone in the family needs to hear how Mom and Dad are honestly affected by his or her behavior.

A typical reaction of parents after their children have moved out is: I wish I had communicated better and more often.

6. Say "I love you." Take your hostile, defiant teenager by the shoulders, square him around, look him in the eye, and say, "I love you and I always will." He may shrug it off and back away, but he needs to hear it. Even if he reacts negatively to that scene, he has to have those words stored in his memory bank.

A young man came home after drinking heavily and staying out all night. His dad put his arms around the boy and said, "Son, I love you, and I am willing to do whatever it takes to deal with your problems. We're in this together."

The boy shrugged his shoulders and went to his room. The next night he came to his dad and said, "I'm ready for help now."

Do it and do it often. If a daughter is cold and distant, she can't afford to have a parent who becomes the same. Do it when it hurts to say it. Do it through eyes of tears if necessary. But get it done. That's what parents with broken hearts say.

"Sometimes it was terribly hard to say," recounted a father from Kansas City. "But I said it. Other times I left a note on his dresser or on the steps to his room. If we were going to argue over everything else, I didn't want there to be any doubt about this."

Often we feel foolish telling someone we love her when she has nothing civil to say to us. She may lie to us, steal from us, embarrass us, cause us pain. And yet we still have to let her know we love her. It's not that we say it every time. That calls for a great deal of stamina. But we must say it enough to make it register.

"I say it every time I write him," a mother declared. "I haven't seen him for a couple of years, but I still write. And I end each letter with, 'Remember, I will always love you,' and I mean it."

7. Show affection. Porcupine teenagers may not like to be hugged. They may be terribly difficult to put our arms around, but many parents wish they had done it more often.

Typically parents become huggers, holders, and even kissers after they have had trouble with one child. Then they determine to embrace every child who is still at home. Clearly they wish they had the rebellious child around to hug. Seeing their lack of affection as a mistake, they have promised themselves not to make it again.

An older boy complained to his parents, "You love my sisters more than you love me, don't you?" His sisters were younger and still in what the parents felt was the cuddly stage. Their son noticed the difference and evidently thought he wasn't too old for a cuddle now and then too.

"My son was standing alone by the kitchen door, his face taut, his shoulders rigid. I could tell his mind was pulling apart, trying to decide whether to obey or to grab the doorknob and run away for another evening. I walked over, lump in my throat, and put one arm around that bubbling volcano. It was the only thing I could do."

Another dad said, "Whenever we get together, my son will give me a hug. He won't say much, but he will give me a hug."

"I'd try to hug him in the morning before he left," a mother added. "He always seemed so down, and a hug was all I could do."

8. Love unconditionally. That's the goal. Sometimes it's just the ideal.

A man who was an alcoholic for thirty years and now has become a Christian is disappointed that his parents didn't accept him unconditionally even when he was drinking so heavily.

In all fairness to his parents, consider what he did. He continuously came home at all hours falling-down drunk. The man stank from booze and urine. Repeatedly he threw up all over the house and wet the bed, couch, and carpets. His behavior hurt his parents' health and drove his brothers and sisters away.

The man wrecked cars, seriously injured a passenger, was repeatedly arrested, rushed into a marriage and then divorced. Frequently he left home and didn't contact his parents for years.

Decades later, he holds it against his parents for not accepting him unconditionally.

That would have been nice, but it's asking a great deal. The question should not be, Can we *accept* children? but rather, Can we *love* them?

This is a tall order to fill. Many parents continue to love unconditionally under the most horrendous of circumstances. That is the best way if they can pull it off. No doubt it is the kind of love God has for his children. No doubt we would all be better off for it. And yet every parent is sympathetic to those who find such love difficult to maintain.

Rather than insist that parents must garner up unconditional love, let us recommend they *try* it. God loves us even in our rebellion. God's love is consistent even when we turn our backs on him. We need to get as close to that kind of love as we can.

On that basis we can begin to deal with unconditional love for our children. Parents with broken hearts are humble enough to know how tough that is.

9. Let your child express anger. Temper outbursts and extreme anger are a shock at first. In some children the hostility begins with the onset of the teen years. Others seem angry even as preschoolers. There is no magic time when young people begin to go into rages.

When parents first see it, they are usually confused. How could their innocent child come to express all of this vile anger? We think it is temporary and will soon pass away. Sometimes we ignore it. At other times we come down hard and demand that they cool it.

Unfortunately, for some families the madness doesn't go away. It might even increase in intensity and in frequency. When this happens, parents often become frightened.

Veteran parents tell us not to be intimidated by the anger. Let them be mad. Parents have to draw lines and set boundaries. Even if their youth resents it and throws fits, the parents cannot afford to remove boundaries.

Young people need to get angry, and adults need to let them. The anger could get out of hand, and the adult may need help from the authorities. But a parent must remain firm and let the youth vent his hostility as long as it is not physically harmful. Ventilation is a hopeful sign that could lead to understanding and resolution.

More than once parents may have to decide whether or not to lock their bedroom door to protect themselves against their own angry child. Many parents are driven to this point. But if we retreat every time a child becomes angry, that child will learn how to frighten and control his own parents.

Parents have to stand up and let their young person be angry.

10. Never hit your adolescent child. Adults who hit adolescents are courting disaster. They have challenged that young person to either hit back or run. Almost never do parents win a physical confrontation. Even if they win the fight, they will almost certainly lose the teenager.

The temptation to hit can become overwhelming, but don't yield. Protect yourself if necessary, but do not hit an adolescent.

11. Tell it like it is. "When Todd was arrested, I went to my Bible study group the next night and told them exactly what had happened. I couldn't cope with the problem and try to cover it up at the same time. I simply didn't have the energy," a father told me.

Often people know more about the situation than we, their parents, know. More people know than we might think. It's best to assume that everyone knows about your child's problem and act accordingly. That doesn't mean we owe everyone an explanation or a detailed account. However, it is usually futile to try and keep a big secret. Remember:

1. You can't keep it a secret.
2. Some people need to know so they can help.
3. You have more important, more immediate things to tend to.

"All I could think of was, what if Grandmother finds out? What if Grandmother finds out? If I had it to do all over again, I'd tell Grandmother the first day," said a lady from the Midwest.

12. Learn to laugh and enjoy life. It's the last thing you feel like doing, but it has to be done. If a parent shuts down and stops living, the situation will degenerate more rapidly. Not only will the parents get hurt, but so will the siblings.

When night comes, the stars are always there. It is only the darkness that allows us to appreciate their glitter.

A young person's defiant lifestyle could last a year or two. On the other hand, his behavior might remain outrageous for a decade or two. For some it might never turn around. In the face of that potential, are we willing to give up all happiness because our child is in a rebellious stage? There are parents who elect never to smile again. They have allowed a bad situation to poison everything around them.

"I felt like a combat chaplain," one father observed. "While everything was blowing up around me, I had to remain calm, cheerful, and optimistic. It's the only way to go."

Some situations we cannot change. We cannot make the bad times into good times. But God has given us the ability to find joy amidst our pain.

Many parents wish they had had a dozen hints when their troubles started. Instead they had to learn everything the hard way. Their hope is that others will benefit from their experience.

Above these dozen bits of advice is one overruling guideline to keep in mind. Both parents and rebellious young people said to be sure and mention this bit of wisdom: *Don't blame yourself.*

Many young people come back to tell their parents that there wasn't anything they could have done. The defiant life was the child's choosing, and he was determined that no one would stop him.

We hurt everyone involved by blaming ourselves. Anyone who tries to affix blame usually ends up making the constructive process more difficult.

The main question to be answered is, Where do we go from here?

Nineteen

Looking for Purpose

called a woman and asked if I could interview her for this book. Her son had been involved in years of rebellious and destructive behavior.

"This may be exactly what I've been looking for," she replied as she began to cry. "I've prayed for years that there might be some purpose to all of this. Maybe God will help others through the book."

The search for purpose is typical among parents with broken hearts. Most were brought up to believe that God has a purpose for everything in life. Believing that the Lord could have intervened at any time, they feel he must have had a reason for not turning their son or daughter around.

"One of my twin daughters died nearly two years ago," a gray-haired gentleman reported. "Don't think I haven't looked almost every day for God's reason for taking her life."

It is a healthy sign when a parent tries to bring something good from the loss and tragedy. The very question suggests that the parent wants to make sense out of life. He or she wants to take a loss and find some way to turn it into a gain. The gain may be for others rather than for himself. The gain will never erase or justify the loss, but the hope is that the disaster will not be a total loss.

Brokenhearted parents also want to reaffirm their belief in God. A terrible disappointment has crashed into their lives, and they want to maintain their faith despite this horror. By asking God for direction and purpose, they continue their decision to walk close to him.

Purpose, meaning, faith, faithfulness, trust, and service are concepts that flood the believer's heart and mind. Parents want to find comfort in their continued dedication to these concepts.

Letting Go of "Why?"

Too often we are bogged down trying to discover the answer to "Why?" The question is normal, but it may get in the way of our ability to accept the facts and find purpose in the future.

"Why did God take her?"
"Why did our son reject our love?"
"Why did she have to marry him?"
"Why didn't God stop my son?"

Usually we look in three directions for an answer to the why question.

1. Why did our child do what he did?
2. Why didn't we do enough to prevent this?
3. Why didn't God intervene?

It is as if a ranch hand kept a horse in a corral only to arise one morning and discover the mare gone. The gate to the corral stands wide open. If the wrangler sits on the trough and asks why the gate was open, he probably is wasting his time. Did the horse learn to work the lever, did I leave the gate ajar, did God open the gate? How long will the wrangler sit around asking "Why?"

The true answer to the question may never be found. And if by some miracle the reason is discovered, what will change? If the wrangler solves the mystery, will the horse return gladly to the corral?

Obviously the answer is no. No amount of soul searching will correct the past. Now that the horse has bolted, the only appropriate question is "What now?"

Asking why it happened becomes a waste of valuable and needed energy. Sometimes we question in an attempt to redo the past. Sometimes we do it to avoid facing the present. And sometimes we do it because we don't know what else to do.

In order to deal with separation and grief, we must let go of the "Why?" Only by moving to the reality of the present will we be able to get hold of our lives and cope with our family's pain.

Separation, loss, and grief are not abnormal. They are not uncommon. Our situation is unique as to its particulars, but not as to its category. All of us suffer loss as part of life, and there is no exact answer to "Why?"

One gentleman who suffered enormous physical pain was asked why this happened to him. "Why not me?" he replied. Why shouldn't injuries, diseases, loss, and pain come to us? Is there some reason why God or destiny or fortune or any other force should have made us exempt from tragedy?

Separation sooner or later is everyone's normal lot. Unfortunately the separation from young people often comes entirely too soon.

Searching for Purpose

Attempting to find meaning and purpose in the events surrounding our broken hearts is a valid goal. Life needs meaning and purpose. The mistake many of us make is looking for purpose in the tragedy itself. Real meaning is found only in our *response* to that tragedy.

A fifteen-year-old boy is killed in a car accident. What is the purpose to be found in that son's death? The answer is none. We shouldn't try to force some magic accomplishment into the death itself.

Some people say the boy died because God was lonely and needed more angels or that God wanted to teach the lad a lesson. Others speculate that God punished the boy or that God knew what kind of hard life he was going to lead and removed him early.

None of these answers is satisfactory.

When a teen is delinquent, some say that God is teaching us patience or preparing us for a rough future. Others say God is testing our faith—as if God would turn the son into a bank robber just to complete the parents' Sunday school lesson.

None of these answers is satisfactory.

There is purpose to be found in the tragedy that comes through our children. The purpose is found in how we handle those events. Pain, agony, heartbreak, disaster, and loss have no meaning. Meaning is discovered by our response to those terrible events.

Read that paragraph again!

If a daughter becomes addicted to drugs, the addiction serves no purpose. It was not good that she used drugs or wrecked her mind and body. That was bad. However, if her awful experience causes us to express our love more, to grow closer to her sisters, or to volunteer at a youth center, purpose has come out of the tragedy.

Many parents facing painful disappointment eventually look for solace to a famous passage of Scripture found in Romans 8:28: "And we know that in all things God works for the good of those who love him, who have been called according to his purpose." Understood correctly this verse addresses our dilemma.

The verse does not assure the reader that all things are good. Some things are lousy, bad, terrible. Paul, the author, is not simply trying to put the best light on everything. Nor is he attempting to comfort the grieving with hollow words.

When bad things happen in our family, God is willing to work those events into something that will be good. God wants to draw gain out of the pain. If we cooperate with God to find the good, we have turned the terrible situation into something that has purpose and meaning.

On the other hand, if we throw up our hands and merely curse the suffering, we intensify the loss. Spirituality in the best sense of the term helps us to turn bad into good. That is God's offer in Romans 8:28.

We cannot expect God to change the past. We do not ask God to tell us the alcoholism, death, or estrangement were really good, but merely disguised. We will not ask God to help us rejoice in our child's arrest.

Rather, we ask God to look for ways to turn the tragedy of the past into some valuable meaning in the future. Only then do we make sense out of the verse and put it to maximum use and relief.

We want to find meaning in suffering. God offers us meaning and purpose in how we respond to that suffering.

On December 12, 1994, Teresa McGovern died on the snow-covered ground in Madison, Wisconsin. Forty-five years old, she lost her battle with alcoholism and died of exposure.

George McGovern, former U.S. Senator and Democratic nominee for president in 1972, spoke freely of his love for the girl who was "a special joy to our family." As an adult, Teresa brought joy to many of her friends and, according to her father, also caused them to share part of her suffering.

As I read McGovern's article, I could hear a brokenhearted father trying to give meaning to her tragedy. Maybe by speaking out he could help other families with sons and daughters in similar situations.

Loss has meaning if we reach out to touch others, if we permit ourselves the strength to grow, or if we find new ways to express love, faith, and caring.

The Compassionate Friends is a prime example. The group consists of parents who have lost a child in death. Its members have bound together to help other parents who have also lost a child. They provide support for parents by newsletters, lending libraries, speakers, support groups, and telephone friends.

Something good has come out of something terrible. That isn't why the terrible thing happened. But it is an attempt to rise up to the next level and see something good come from it.

Giving Ourselves Time

Not everyone is ready for this message. Some of us remain fixed entirely on the loss for a long time. A mother might spend ten years concentrating on her defiant daughter's continued deviant lifestyle. Every day she might torture herself over the child's failure to straighten out and turn around.

That parent isn't ready. She continues to drown in the misery. If a life preserver is thrown to her, that parent will choose to reject it.

A man in Louisville visits the grave of his teenage son once a day. This father has made daily trips for over five years. He isn't ready. He doesn't want to hear about meaning, purpose, love, or today. In a way his life ended when his son's car crossed over that yellow line. He isn't ready to go on.

Moving on to purpose is a conscious decision. No one is likely to steal our grief away from us if we choose to stay at that level.

For some parents all they have left of their rebellious, defiant child is the grief that accompanies his actions. The young man shows no sign of changing his attitude and treating his parents in a civil, loving way. The parents feel that the only part of their son that they can successfully hold onto is the rebellious side. If someone tells them to back up and snap out of this, the parents believe the final thread of relationship is threatened. They believe that to lose the suffering would be to lose time.

Each of us must decide that it is time to move on. We have to accept the fact that looking for the good will neither desecrate the memory of our child, nor erase any contact with our wild child. Moving on only adds meaning to other relationships.

The message isn't, Forget your child and get on with life. The better message is, Accept the pain for what it is and rise up to make something good happen.

We aren't all public speakers, group leaders, or writers. Nor do we need to be. Purpose might be found in the new way we treat the other children. Meaning could be expressed in our relationship with the grandchildren. The good could be realized in the parents' renewed love for each other.

No one should try to limit the good that God will be able to work out with our cooperation and dedication. There must be as many ways to carry out meaning as there are stars in the sky.

Willing and aware are the key attitudes. We will not permit pain to drive us into retreat. Eventually we are determined, by God's grace, to turn our energies around and lead the charge back into life.

Pain and loss are not the biggest waste. But pain and loss that don't result in some form of good are indeed total emptiness.

None of us should be surprised, however, if it takes a while before we can begin to turn our loss into meaning. It takes time to accept our loss. It takes time to adjust to the sad facts. We have been wounded. Those wounds will need time and help so they can begin to heal. Only as the healing takes place will we be able to identify the good we might create.

We don't walk out of the jail, the hospital, the mortuary, and look for a new mission. The hurt might be too great to ever imagine that we would want to trust or to get involved again. But with the healing will come new energy and new direction, and we will feel far more like pursuing it.

Twenty

Eating Pudding Pies

A person who now has diabetes used to enjoy apple pies. When his medical problem was discovered, he had to give up those delicious pies. At first he complained and felt sorry for himself.

As time went by, the diabetic discovered sugar-free pudding pies. Granted, they weren't apple pies, but after a while the adjustment went fairly well.

Today this person knows he will probably never be able to eat regular apple pies. And he still misses them. But he has decided to lick his lips and enjoy pudding pies as if they were delicacies from the finest ovens.

Tomorrow will be different for each broken-hearted parent. A few will never see their child again. Others will be reunited with bonds that are stronger than ever. Most of us will be somewhere in the middle. Our relationship to our child will be a mixture of highs and lows, of enthusiasm and pain.

Most of us will learn to eat the pie that is set before us. We will enjoy what we can have and stop cursing what we cannot have.

Frustrated, hurt, and disappointed, we will now decide to go on and accept all the good gifts that God sends our way. We will enjoy whatever family relationship we can pull together. We will be glad to reach out and participate even on a limited scale. And by the grace of God, we will make the most of anything we can have.

Life will go on. We will meet new people, help those who need us, and develop new relationships. We will praise God, serve him, and ask for more wisdom.

Out of serious setback and genuine pain we will rise up to grasp each day. And the day will bring us new satisfaction because we decided to reach for all it has to offer.

Sharing with Others

With most tragedies we find the strength to go on by sharing our experiences with others in need. Millions of parents have had their hearts broken. The majority keep the story to themselves and never receive help. If more of us would open up and tell others what we have experienced, many parents could have their burdens lifted dramatically.

This isn't an easy subject to discuss. It isn't like fly-fishing, baseball, or handcraft. There are risks involved and agonies to relive. We can understand anyone's reluctance to hang it out on the clothesline of life.

But healing comes by sharing. It also comes by listening. Whenever two people can share and listen, they have the full potential of rising above their wounds.

Find an avenue to express your pain. By expressing it, the sharpness will diminish for both the speaker and the receiver.

Finding Spiritual Strength

The Old Testament prophets looked for a Messiah who would eventually come and "bind up the brokenhearted" (Isa. 61:1). Jesus told us that this passage of Scripture has now been fulfilled (Luke 4:16–21). To this day it remains a major part of the ongoing ministry of Jesus Christ.

His invitation includes parents who have known suffering within their own families. Increasingly we acknowledge our need for spiritual strength as we plow our way through life. That spiritual strength can be found by depending on Christ and the Holy Spirit in terribly trying times.

Spirituality will give us a sense of belonging, a feeling of outside power, a knowledge that someone larger than us actually cares, a forgiving spirit, a wider perspective, an attitude of tolerance, purpose in life, someone to talk to, quiet moments of guidance, courage to rise above circumstances, and much more. Spiritual strength is more than a slogan, and many professional caregivers have come to accept that reality.

True spirituality teaches us that if apple pie is taken away from us, we should go after pudding pie as if it were a delicacy. We must concentrate on what we have, instead of brooding over what we do not have.

Thankfulness helps us rise up and take on the day with all of its challenges, gifts, and goodness. We can thank God for every ray of sunshine that comes our way.

William L. Coleman is a best-selling author and an authority on family living. He travels extensively to speak at conferences and seminars. He can be contacted through Revell Publishers.

~~Is~~ Absolute Truth User Friendly

·Introductions

    Who

        # of children. + What do they

        hope they get out of class.

~~Children in X~~ Generation

LAUNCHERS

    Why haven't they launched.

    In What Way Have They

    NOT Launched.

Definition. Usually have

children between 18 &

30 - still dependent in

some way on parents

Navigating to New Worlds of Volunteering

Attitudes
Extended Adolescents

Child   Parent

Live Hard - Die Fast
Leave
~~Live~~ a good looking corpse.

Healthy life.   Mind altering
   Live in Gym.   drugs.
Can control

Just Do it   Need motivation

Low Key - Non Agression.   Aggressive Gobetter
Difficult - Make Decisions   Think Big - Make
                              Decisions

Jobs means to   Work Long Hrs.
  an end.   to achieve Goal
Take jobs to
buy electronic equip

Resent Boomers for   Frustrated
  ~~taking~~ all good job   ~~all~~ work
                      ethic.

·· Redefine relationships   Destroyed
   Latch Key Kids   relationships
                             Free Love.
                             Abortion
                             Delayed Child
13640   Lo   Bearing